Will NoSky

Return Delivery

Creative Science Fiction from Will NoSky:

Privateer Captain Jennifer Bane novels:

FORCED DELIVERY (#1)

Privateer Captain Jennifer Bane finds out that children are dying due to lack of medicine. Then she learns people are remarkably reversing their ages on her home planet of Markem. The key was to uncover the linkage before more people died or the opposition party on Markem used their 'youth for all' promise to destroy democracy.

Sure, Jennifer had heard about telepaths that could kill with thought. She'd just never gone up against them before—until now.

Former enemies haunt her and the possibility of love tricks her into believing she can be happy and still know the truth. But she can't, because the truth is the worst outcome of all…

FRAGILE DELIVERY (#2)

When Privateer Captain Jennifer Bane's fiancé is kidnapped, she is injured and unable to rescue him alone. Accustomed to being the lone apex predator, Jennifer has to let the people that care about her find him. With the help of her two sworn vassals, and the two women she rescued from a defiled life of slavery, they join forces. It's pack predation this time, the best way to hunt what you're trying to catch.

No longer about finding one man, it's a race to end the cruelty created by beings without morals. To stop genetics for profit. To destroy a resort that's hunting beings for sport.

RETURN DELIVERY (#3)

ONE

In time, the child's life she saved would be what she remembered, not the bloodied body on the deck.

Jennifer Bane watched the riot start earlier in the day. The throng had taken on a surging life of its own spreading out from the Crossings, which was the center atrium of Biltmire Space Station. More angry people joined the emboldened hordes spilling into all four concourses of the station.

"Watch out!" Jennifer yelled by reflex, yanking the small hand of a six-year-old boy toward her. A lethal laser blade knife was flying through the air headed directly at the child and his father standing next to him.

The boy's frightened eyes locked onto Jennifer's as the weapon hit home, slicing his father's head diagonally from the top of his left ear, down through his lips, and out the opposite side of his neck.

Jennifer pulled the boy's face into her stomach just in time to cover his eyes from the horror. Blood sprayed the boy's back.

The boy's father toppled in the direction of the falling laser blade. The body followed the deadly shank to the deck. Jennifer's eyes landed on what she had shielded the boy from— his father's head was sliced diagonally in two.

A blur of movement jabbed her peripheral vision. It was different from the mob of people all around her. Jennifer blinked, not certain she saw any motion at all. As soon as it happened it darted back into the jostling crowd like mist shot from a gun. The laser blade was on the deck in front of her, then it wasn't.

The boy tried to free himself from her grasp but she tensed her right hand pulling his face back into her stomach. When she looked down at the boy she was shocked to see that the laser blade was now in her left hand.

Just then Jennifer was blindsided from behind, both she and the boy tackled, her landing on top of him with a low grunt. The laser blade was yanked from her grasp then her wrists pulled behind her tie-wrapped painfully together. The boy struggled to get out from under her. Jennifer was picked up forcibly by two station security guards then a third guard snatched up the child in his arms, turned quick, followed by Jennifer being frog marched along behind.

The guard holding the boy peeled off fast. A brief glance backward by the guard landed on Jennifer's eyes. The man's look said *I want to get him as far away from you as possible.*

Not two minutes later, Jennifer was marched through one, then another, sliding hatchway into the heart of Biltmire Space Station Detention. Her head was on a swivel, her senses piqued to a fevered pitch. She studied every lock, latch, hatchway, surveillance vid cam, and angle of the corridor. Jennifer's instincts took over instructing the hammering heart in her chest to feed more blood to her brain to process, sort, analyze and store everything her eyes collected.

One of the detention guards stepped up to the control station hatch and pressed the comm button above the scan pad.

"Prisoner intake," he said.

The other guard pushed Jennifer, then a sliding hatch further down the corridor swooshed aside. Jennifer flicked a glance at the control station room as she passed. The lurking detention guard stared back through the thick synth glass window, moving a hand that had activated the sliding hatch to the interview room up ahead. The guard shoved Jennifer into the square little room; the hatch closed behind her.

The interview room hatch opened less than a minute later, and a tall sergeant wearing a dark uniform jacket and trousers stepped through parking herself in front of Jennifer as the hatch closed. She was a stick of a woman, with hollow cheeks, and skin that clung to her face outlining every bony contour. Her hair was an unremarkable shade of light brown tucked up under the requisite Station Security Detention blue beret. The older woman's dark eyes bore down on Jennifer who was seated in the only chair at a small dura steel table.

"Jennifer Bane, you are bound by law for murder and attempted kidnapping. Using the riot to hide your intent didn't work," the sergeant said sharply. The anger in her tone seemed to cleave to her like the lines worn into her skin.

Undeterred, the first of several things on Jennifer's mind washed across her face in waves of concern.

"Is the boy okay? Please tell me he doesn't know what happened to his father?" Her dark green eyes searched the sergeant's face for the answer.

The sergeant tensed, her body refusing to offer any comfort.

"Why should you care?"

The sergeant's question hurt, as intended. However, Jennifer was not naïve. She knew why she had been detained. At 33 years old, she had been through a lot and seen even more. She had been a Privateer Space Captain up until 20 months ago when she took a forced sabbatical to protect her health.

The question as to how the laser blade ended up in her hand was not solvable at the moment. This didn't panic her in the least. She'd made enemies in the past and was quite aware of their tendency to show up in her life when least expected. Immediate action was what Jennifer plotted now. Being tied up and incarcerated was not going to help solve this problem. If anything, Jennifer felt sorry for the sergeant for what was going to happen shortly.

Since it was obvious the sergeant was not going to answer her question, Jennifer made a quick decision about what to do next, as much by instinct as necessity.

"Pen to write with and old fashioned synth pap, Sergeant."

It wasn't a demand, but a request. She sat stoically, and stared straight ahead.

The sergeant considered her request as much as she seemed to be considering her. She knew who Jennifer was. It would be all but impossible not to know. Jennifer Bane was engaged to the Biltmire Space Station Director Krachalavito Bantor. It was quite possible that this sergeant had served with Krachy Bantor. Bantor was a member of Station Security (Sta Sec) over three years ago before becoming Space Station Director. The sergeant looked old enough without doubt.

Not liking the inevitable rights of her captive, the sergeant decided to thrust one more put-down at Jennifer before she left. The satisfaction in her delivery was unmistakable.

"You won't be getting married tomorrow as planned, Bane."

She spat then turned and left the room. The sergeant knew she had to give Jennifer a way to communicate with the outside world. Writing down a request on synth pap or using a hand comp to call someone was a detained person's legal right.

Jennifer didn't flinch even though the thought of letting down the man she loved tomorrow upset her deeply. At the moment, one of her main concerns was the growing pain stopping the blood flow to her hands. The plasti tie wrap had been pulled tight. She worked to control her breathing and heart rate. The collated data she'd gathered on her brief trip to the interview room was already parsed, labeled, prioritized, and stored for quick retrieval. Smiling thinly, Jennifer knew she didn't miss any detail about the layout and workings of the detention center. It calmed her to know that she would be using that information soon.

Jennifer was six feet tall and thin. She wore a blue long sleeve crew neck form-fitting shirt over straight leg black trousers. Her hair was sandy brown done up in a tousled lob cut framing her thin face. Best of all in a situation like this, she was fit. Fitness had always aided her ability to stand up to the rigors of her profession, and being fit boosted her defense against the relentless chase of complicated obstacles that followed her no matter how hard she tried to outrun them. Jennifer would get through the next few hours; she always did.

Her next decision was a difficult one, but essential. She began corkscrewing her wrists stretching the limits of the tie wrap. The rising pain did not register on her face, and Jennifer was not frightened about the outcome. Twisting her wrists dug the sharp edges into the skin on the top of her wrists. That was why she was not afraid. When the cord cut through her skin, the incisions would not open up the bottom-side radial arteries. Even if it could, there was not a high probability she would die because the vessel walls or blood clotting in a healthy person like her was not degraded. Also, the tie wrap would not slit the arteries lengthwise, but crosswise instead.

Just then, Jennifer began to feel the blood on the top of her wrists flow. The sharp edges of the tie wrap had ruptured the ulnar arteries in both wrists. The blood flow began to pick up speed, dripping onto the chair then down to the deck. She didn't know how long it would be until the next person came into the interview room, so she stopped the arduous corkscrewing movements satisfied that enough blood would be visible when the time came. A security vid cam was not allowed in the room. Private conversations had to take place with the detainee and their legal representative. Jennifer waited.

It didn't take long, and by then a decent sized pool of blood had gathered on the deck behind her. The hatch opened, the sergeant stalked through, the hatch slid closed. A small pad of synth pap was clutched in her hand. She tossed it on the table and eyed Jennifer disdainfully happy to let her suffer in the tie wrap longer. The sergeant finally angled around the small table to cut the tie wrap. As she rounded the table her boot strike landed in the blood.

The woman snorted an uninterested breath.

"Faking an injury isn't going to buy you out of this, Bane."

Her left hand gripped Jennifer's bicep and jerked her standing. The two women were the same height. The hateful woman turned her head sideways whispering in Jennifer's ear.

"I could leave and let you bleed out, no vid cam..." Her eyes flicked toward the ceiling and back, the corners of her craggy, downturned lips rising into a sneer.

Jennifer eased the chair back with her legs to straighten, then turned to face Hollow Cheeks.

"No guts, no greatness. I double-dog dare you, Sergeant."

Jennifer's green eyes scanned the women distastefully head to toe and back.

"Still only a Sergeant. Pity, but chicken shit is chicken shit at any age." Jennifer's smile held no warmth.

Hollow Cheeks was torn, but not torn about her feelings, not at all. She was the type of person that lived in a constant state of annoyed. Annoyed she was still working detention, annoyed she wasn't getting married too, annoyed at all the extra work the effin' riot caused. She wanted to gut punch Jennifer bad and leave her to wither.

It was written all over Hollow Cheek's face. Jennifer seized the opening.

"I'll even relax my abs," Jennifer dipped her eyes down at her stomach, "free shot, Butch. C'mon, give in, why deny yourself the pleasure?"

Hollow Cheeks didn't, deny herself the pleasure that is. Her right hook was expertly delivered. Of the few things this sergeant could do, proper punching technique was at the top of the short list. Her waist and hips turned powering her small, boney fist dead center into Jennifer's diaphragm.

Good thing Jennifer lied. The impact doubled her over. If not for tense muscles, Jennifer's head would have surely smacked the tabletop. That would have been far worse than the punch. Jennifer had a history of concussions. The last concussion eight months ago was very bad indeed.

Gasping for breath, Jennifer stayed doubled over longer than necessary. The rage was still building within Hollow Cheeks. It hadn't dissipated much in the ten, now approaching thirty, full seconds Jennifer stayed bent over catching her breath. Jennifer was acting as much as anything. Yes, it hurt like hell, but the goal here was distraction, carelessness, and complacency. Jennifer's plan was thin, but included all these wrinkles. As focused as she was, Jennifer could not deny that there was going to be *some* pleasure in the inevitable outcome.

Not able to wait any longer, Hollow Cheeks forgot about legal rights. She took a step back and shot her hand down grabbing the back of Jennifer's neck. She jerked Jennifer standing. Hollow Cheeks knocked the chair over with her knee. At the same time she grabbed Jennifer's bicep and pulled her around the table hesitating at the hatch. She bent at the waist to pass her chest over the scan pad to open the hatch. Her security key card was in the breast pocket.

Out into the corridor Hollow Cheeks felt Jennifer tense, fighting against being led down the hall to the nurse's station past the control station. Jennifer's resistance pissed off Hollow Cheeks even more, but she couldn't take out her anger on Jennifer now because vid cams and other guards would see. Blood continued to drip behind Jennifer as the two of them approached the nurse's station up ahead. Jennifer leaned back digging her heels into the deck with each step. Hollow Cheek jabbed angry looks at her time and again.

The riot on-station was keeping detention busy. The duo sidestepped several guards escorting other detainee's down the corridor in the opposite direction. Hollow Cheeks yanked Jennifer to a halt in front of the nurse station hatch then dropped her grip on Jennifer's arm. The sergeant pushed the comm button above the scan pad.

"Prisoner triage, prisoner triage," she bellowed into the small comm above the scan pad. The deadbolt on the hatch snapped and the hatch swooshed aside. Hollow Cheeks didn't try to explain anything to the nurse in the room; she just shoved Jennifer past the threshold.

When Jennifer turned quick on a heel to face Hollow Cheeks, blood windmilled out away from her wrists in a colorful little arc spraying a neat line of crimson across the legs of the nurse to her left. The woman's eyes shot open, but she said nothing. Jennifer eyed Hollow Cheeks casually, her mouth curved into a sneer, and shot her an air kiss smiling evilly as the hatch slid shut.

Still steaming mad, Hollow Cheeks hated she had to wait in the corridor for Jennifer to be treated. She just couldn't control the hate planted in her chest for everything that was happening today. Truth be told, Hollow Cheeks wanted to join all the rioters protesting Station Security's lack of progress on the crime of the decade. That was the sole reason the riot started earlier. People were fed up with no arrests, no solid leads, and the knowledge that the serial killer on station was still at large. His latest victim had been murdered just this morning. It was the bastard's eleventh. The riot started because people were furious that the serial killer had not been caught.

Jennifer submitted to treatment with inward gratitude. It felt wonderful having the tie wrap cut free from her throbbing wrists. When the nurse washed the incisions then applied a line of clear, soothing, quick-heal gel across each cut, Jennifer sighed. She did not, however, let herself retreat into complacency. She had aimed that condition elsewhere. Just like Jennifer's decision to inflict the wrist wounds, the delay tactic of being in the nurse's station was having the desired affect. Hollow Cheeks was an easy target in her professional opinion.

Even as the nurse finished up her triage, Jennifer was planted firmly in her own mind's eye. The distance between upcoming action and her physical body in the room was closer than it had been since she arrived in detention. She didn't hear the nurse's comment.

"What was that, nurse?" Jennifer shifted part of her attention on the middle-aged woman.

The nurse's eyes were tired.

"That does it. Get up," she instructed, and moved toward the hatch.

"I'm going to take a leak." Jennifer hopped off the exam table and stepped over to the head in the corner without waiting for permission. Down came her trousers and she lowered her backside.

The nurse turned away and heaved a stuttered sigh trying to control her impatience. It had been a helluva day and it wasn't over. She crossed her arms over her chest taking the brief opportunity to relax for a few uninterrupted seconds. When the nurse didn't hear urine splashing, she poked an angry look at Jennifer.

"You're done, let's go!" She barked, and stepped in Jennifer's direction to speed things along.

"Almost there," Jennifer held up a hand milking the time she spent in the room to its impending maximum.

"I said you're done—get up!" The now angry nurse hovered over her and reached down to grab Jennifer's arm.

The impending time arrived. Jennifer pushed herself to her feet, wincing at the pain in her stomach. She pulled up her trousers. When the hatch moved out of the way, Hollow Cheek's back was to the room. Jennifer watched the agitated woman's shoulders heave up and down with frustration. Jennifer didn't smile inwardly at the success of this wrinkle. Instead she was scanning the scene beyond with hyper intensity. The time to act was drawing close.

Hollow Cheeks swiveled, pulling Jennifer by the arm straight ahead. To the left was a railing looking down into the detention pod. Cells lined the second floor they were on as well as the lower level. They both passed the backside of the control station to their right.

Feeling began to return to Jennifer's hands, and the quick-heal gel was already pulling the skin tight across the ragged incisions on her wrists.

Jennifer glanced to see yet another detainee being brought through the entry hatch she had come through earlier. The woman guard holding the prisoner said, "Prisoner intake," into the comm above the scan pad next to the hardened hatch of the control station.

Hollow Cheeks pushed Jennifer down the length of the balcony, then down the stairs, which brought them to a closed cell on the first floor.

"Open one oh nine," Hollow Cheeks ordered as she pushed the comm button next to the cell hatch. A few seconds later the hatch moved out of the way.

Wrinkle accomplished, so far. Jennifer's body was rigid. The instant she and Hollow Cheeks stepped into the cell, Jennifer's right arm bolted from her side shedding the grip. She extended the arm into the crease of the jacket lapel opening on Hollow Check's chest then twisted in the opposite direction, using the coiled momentum of her waist. She unleashed a full powered round-house elbow into Hollow Cheek's nose. The elbow-to-nose smack echoed in the small cell. Her right arm continued its journey through the front of Hollow Cheek's coat and into the arm of her jacket. On Hollow Cheek's way down to the deck, the side of her head caught the lower bunkbed support with another audible crack. By then Hollow Cheek's arm had slipped out of her jacket replaced by Jennifer's arm. Jennifer pulled the jacket off the unconscious woman, then shrugged it on straitening it out flat in front. She bent down, grabbed the beret on the deck, snatched the key card from Hollow Cheek's breast pocket along with a tie wrap she found in the second trouser pocket she searched. Jennifer stood grimacing at her sore stomach. Little time had been waisted, and a small bit of pleasure *was* a part of the inevitable end to Hollow Cheek's day.

The woman sitting on the top bunk snickered.

"Text book," the woman said with a hint of admiration.

Jennifer looked up at her.

"Ya think?" The tiny chrono in her head was ticking into the future.

"Loud, if nothing else. Frog Face had a hard head." The spindly woman jumped down off the bunk landing in front of Jennifer. "Can I help?"

"Yes, prisoner transfer. You game?" Jennifer motioned for the woman to step closer.

The woman nodded, turned and let Jennifer pull the tie wrap around her wrists.

"Hold a sec..." Jennifer tucked her hair under the beret so it would resemble Hollow Cheek's exposed hair line. She grabbed the woman's arm pulling her out of the cell then pressed the comm button.

"Close one oh nine." After the hatch closed, the two woman climbed the stairs.

"Submissive and slwoah," Jennifer slurred the last word.

Jennifer knew her health problems were showing up at the worst possible time. The gut punch, the neck jerk, or the round-house elbow, triggered the symptoms. Whatever it was, the grade 3 concussion Jennifer suffered eight months ago was with her again, *oh no...*

As if on queue, her symptoms elevated. She stumbled sideways into the woman at the top of the stairs.

The woman flicked a glance at Jennifer and, somehow, knew she was getting sick. She shuffled tight to Jennifer's side pressing her spinner-like body into her. The woman's hand grabbed Jennifer's wrist for support. The close body contact helped. Jennifer took in several deep breaths and was able to make the right turn down the second-floor balcony toward the control station.

Thankfully, there was not a logjam at the comm button next to the control station hatch. This was very little comfort though. When Spinner Babe let go of Jennifer's wrist, some of the fresh quick-heal gel pulled free. Blood started dripping from the cut.

Now at the comm button, Jennifer didn't know the proper procedure to transfer a prisoner. Should she use the comm button to ask permission or should she use Hollow Cheek's key card on the exit hatches?

Spinner Babe nodded at the comm button. Jennifer saw it and pushed the button, "Prisoner transfer," she said. The hatch behind them started moving aside.

The two women stepped through the hatch when a voice behind them asked, "Nace, you okay? You're bleeding."

Hollow Cheek's name was Nace Notchins.

Fight or flight?

Or.....become Hollow Cheeks? Worth a try, "Piss off. Little blood don't matter." Jennifer's words tried to imitate the grating voice of Nace Notchins, the hollow cheeked bitch.

The man watched the first hatch close. The hatch had to close before the second hatch, the exit from detention, could open. He shrugged; then he did a double-take.

The guard stepped over to the closed hatch and pounded on the thick synth glass window trying to get Nace's attention. He watched the two women leave detention out the exit hatch with no look back.

The noise of the riot, a good distance down the Security Concourse Street to the left, was loud. Still sick, Jennifer clinched her jaw by reflex; then when the blaring detention escape siren behind her went off, she threw both hands to her ears. The earsplitting stop-and-go horn added to the white noise from the riot and rattled Jennifer's brain.

The guard that saw fake Guard Notchins leave with the prisoner had not been fooled.

TWO

The sound of the escape siren ensured that the detention center exit hatch that Jennifer had just used would open at any second. Then, Jennifer's eyes landed on something that made her gasp. Her hands dropped from both ears unconsciously.

On the other side of the concourse street, hanging from wires affixed to the third story balcony railing, were four men. The dead, naked bodies hung upside-down by an ankle, one man without a head between his shoulders.

Eight station security guards exited from the conspicuous entrance to Sta Sec HQ to Jennifer's right and were jogging toward the suspended bodies dangling high above on the other side of the street.

Spinner Babe shot a hard elbow into Jennifer. The woman didn't know it hurt like hell.

"We've got a window, let's go!"

Spinner Babe pumped her legs with Jennifer falling in behind. The tie wrap Jennifer affixed to the woman was loose. Spinner Babe pulled her wrists out, turned at the waist, and grabbed at the jacket Jennifer was wearing. Jennifer shed the jacket, threw off the beret, and sprinted.

Spinner Babe blended pretty well; she had on grey paints and a long sleeve shirt. Just then the detention center exit hatch behind them opened; three guards spilled out and scanned the concourse street. This is also when the crowd of rioters pushed forward en masse from all sides of the street up ahead.

The loud shouts of defiance turned into outraged screams of anger when dozens of rioters got a glimpse of the hanging bodies for the first time. The numerous Sta Sec guards that were trying to contain the rioters retreated, met up with their eight fellow guards that had exited Sta Sec HQ, and decided there was no way they could contain the horde any longer. They all turned to run for their lives, sprinting hard, for the safety of Sta Sec HQ.

The three detention guards pursuing the two escapees hesitated when their eyes landed on the bodies suspended from the third floor balcony high above. Then they too glanced left, wide-eyed to see the riot mob surging forward. The decision made for them, the three retreated in haste back the way they'd come scrambling to get through the detention center hatch to safety.

By now, Jennifer and Spinner Babe had met up with the rioters. The two women hugged the left wall of the street in an attempt to skirt the crowd. Jennifer pulled Spinner Babe into an alcove between two store fronts and shouted.

"Wait! I need to catch my breath!" Her stomach was killing her.

Spinner Babe was shoved from behind into Jennifer. The two women were chest to chest in the small space.

Spinner Babe threw a hand to the back of her head for protection. She gritted her teeth.

"We can't stay here!" She yelled.

The light entering their small cubbyhole dimmed. A six-foot-six blonde-haired man shoved his girth into the alcove behind Spinner Babe blocking the light. His amiable smile landed on Jennifer as she looked up.

"Perhaps I can be of some assistance ladies!" He shouted.

Jennifer's face could not have held a broader grin.

"Ian!" She yelped, thrilled to see her former starship First Officer and friend Ian McKivey.

Hellos over in an instant, Ian watched the smile drop off Jennifer's face and her eyes explode open, but for some reason Ian didn't turn or react to what Jennifer saw behind him. An arm shot up from behind Ian's back and snatched the incoming dura steel pipe headed for the back of Ian's head.

Ian jabbed his head to the right to signal he was about to head that way. He had heard the impact of the incoming pipe-missile smack the hand of the man watching his six.

"Dimitiri's with me. Let's go!"

Dimitri Volodya was Jennifer's guardian. He was her fealty sworn Pinaten vassal bound by kinship tie to live or die by her command. Right now, he was also living up to his obligation to protect and defend her life.

"My Lord!" Dimitri motioned. "This way!"

Ian wrapped an arm around the two women. He pulled them out from the alcove then took up position behind Spinner Babe, Jennifer next, and Dimitri led the way. Dimitri used the dura steel pipe to cross-check people out of his way.

Ian leaned over doing the best he could to shelter the two women. The four-person pack began to pick up speed. The mob of rioters started to move across the street focusing its anger on Station Security HQ.

Jennifer's wrist began to bleed more. As she grabbed at the wound, another painful yelp erupted from her throat when Dimtiri stopped abruptly.

Dimitri bent down over a wounded rioter wedged against the left street wall. He looked up over his shoulder at Jennifer.

"It looks bad!"

Jennifer read the look in his eyes: *We can't leave her.* Jennifer nodded giving Dimitri permission to help.

In a heave, Dimitri had the woman up over his shoulder in a fireman's carry. He held the pipe with his free hand and started moving again.

The injured woman stirred, the blood from a gash on her forehead spitting rhythmically with each heart beat. Jennifer reached up with her hand and cupped it across the bloody gouge, then closed her fingers tight to help stem the leak.

The woman's blood mixed with her own and streamed down Jennifer's arm.

The rioters were fewer now, having just so many in number, and the bulk of that number were now behind Jennifer's pack. Up ahead on the left street bulkhead were docking hatches. Jennifer knew that all her friends were on-station for her wedding. Her fiancé, space station director Krachy Bantor, had arranged for the three ships that made up the bulk of the wedding party to dock next to each other. The next docking blast hatch they passed was one of those docking slips.

Ian spoke loudly into a hand comp.

Up ahead one of the docking blast hatches moved aside. The five-person-pack hurried inside; the hatch closed behind them.

***

There was no choice but to undock the ship Jennifer boarded and leave the space station. Biltmire Station Security would regroup soon, riot or not, and they would not forget about the mess Jennifer left in her wake. Krachy Bantor may have been the director of the space station, but even his fiancée was not above the law.

Jennifer lay semi-reclined on the operating table in the small Medico aboard her Astra Class Light Cruiser *Viper II*. The ship still belonged to her. Twenty months ago she had leased it to her crew when she took a leave from privateering.

A twenty-something woman poked her head around the open hatchway door jamb.

"Hey," she smiled.

"Hey, Sami. Come in." Jennifer smiled back.

Sami moved to Jennifer's side and by reflex extended a hand that Jennifer took. Sami looked over at the doctor on the other side of the table.

"She giving you any problems, Russ?"

Russell Sauchen was one of Jennifer's oldest friends and her doctor. The portly middle-aged man frowned.

"No, but if she does, I have just the thing to take the bite out of her."

Sami squeezed Jennifer's hand before letting go.

"Good, I thought she may have asked you if she could hop back on-station to get married tomorrow."

"She actually listens to me sometimes."

Sami huffed. "I'll believe it when I see it."

Jennifer often needed to be told what was best for her because her temper had always been a problem, and at times, a noxious problem. "I'm listening. I will."

Russell's look turned serious. "I haven't seen you in a couple of years, Jennifer. I hope you've changed enough to be a good patient. You were lucky today."

"I promise." The fact that she let down Krachy hurt more than her wrists and stomach. She meant what she just said. Jennifer knew that Russell was not going to talk about the results of the brain scan he'd done until Sami left the room.

Sami started to leave. "Good, I think I believe that. You're trainable no matter what Ian says."

"Don't believe everything McKivey tells you. You ought to know that," Jennifer said.

Sami shook her head. "Fighting it, always fighting it aren't you, Jennifer?" She left out the hatch.

Jennifer shook her head. Her head was clear, and it felt fine. Russell had seen to that. She looked up at him.

"She's right, you know."

He stepped over to an exam table and lifted a 3D scan. Holding the holographic brain scan, he strode over to the hatch, waved a hand over the scan pad, and turned as it closed. The lights in the room dimmed.

"The slurred speech is a new symptom, isn't it, Jennifer?"

She nodded.

"The nausea, lack of coordination, balance issues, have you had these episodes before?"

"Yes"

"How long?"

"About two months…"

"You sleeping well?"

"Not really, no."

"Memory problems, any significant head trauma since being blindsided right before Krachy was kidnapped eight months ago?"

"No, no signifiant head trauma since then. I forget things sometimes. I have to write things down to remember them. I even asked the detention sergeant for some synth pap," she shrugged, thinking back to her arrest. "I asked the sergeant by reflex, I guess."

"Before you took her out. Right?"

"Yes, but before that she slugged me in the gut. I wrenched my neck to stop my face from smashing into a table. After that, I planted a hard back-elbow to her face. I was thinking the combination of the two could have triggered all my symptoms."

"That's possible, Jennifer. Let me ask you this—do you get mood swings, short temper?"

Her brows rose, "No more than usual." Her feeble attempt at humor fell flat.

Russell waited.

"I get upset more than I used to. Krachy lets me get away with it, but I know it's starting to piss him off. I even try hiding my slurred speech, but he's seen me do it. I can see the worry in his eyes…It sucks that I'm so damn stubborn that I try to hide shit from him. Not a good road map for an upcoming marriage is it, Russ?"

"No."

Her attention shifted to the 3D scan.

"What we're seeing here," Russell pointed, "this red area, is amyloid plaque buildup." The view was from top down. The ovular shape of Jennifer's skull had red areas near the periphery, and a few toward the center, of her skull. There were at least six distinct blotches.

"This is toxic, Jennifer. And it's quite significant. What you see here would normally indicate early stages of Alzheimer's. Your episodes today, the nausea, balance problem, and sensitivity to sound, tells me you're suffering from post concussion syndrome. Head trauma, of a cumulative nature. You know I hope you have a very long life, but this is a serious condition. This can lead to full on memory loss, deep depression, even suicidal thoughts. Have you ever...?"

Jennifer grabbed the bridge of her nose and snapped her eyes shut. Her eyes opened.

"No, I mean...No, just the stuff I told you about. So, is there a drug I can take?"

Russell turned and placed the 3D scan on the exam table. The lights came up as he turned back around.

"I can prescribe a specific treatment for the nausea and balance issues. But no, the condition itself, there's no drugs. Just take care of your mind. Avoid loud noises, no head trauma at all."

He thinned his lips.

"Don't beat anyone up or get beaten up. Avoid anything strenuous on your head, rough sports, loud concerts. Any more stresses like you had today, and this is going to get worse."

Jennifer searched his face. She didn't find what she was looking for so she asked.

"What did you and Ian discuss? It took you a while to get back in here after you treated the injured woman we brought back with us."

"Are you strong enough to hear it, Jennifer?"

"Are you trying to scare me or what?"

"You should be scared."

"What do you mean?"

"I want to start with a question for you. This is important. When you exited detention, were the four bodies moving, swaying, when you first spotted them hanging way up there, off the balcony?"

That was an odd question, and she had to think hard about the answer. Jennifer tried to put herself back to that moment in time. When Spinner Babe gave her an elbow in the side, she wondered why she had not seen the hanging bodies the second she exited detention. Then it hit her.

"They had just jerked to a stop as though all four bodies had been thrown over the balcony railing seconds before, Russ. I remember now. The bodies were moving, but still had not come to rest. Why is that important?"

"Ian thinks it was a warning, Jennifer."

"A warning?

"Jennifer, Ian believes the serial killer was warning you not to look for him."

"That can't be it. I'm not law enforcement on that statio—"

"—That's not what the warning is about. Let me back up. This was the serial killer's second attempt to stop you from finding out who or what they are. You were framed for murder and kidnapping. You said the laser blade ended up in your hand after you saved the little boy. The laser blade was planted there. You were arrested so that you would be out of the way. When you escaped, the moment you stepped through the detention center exit hatch, they strung the bodies down in front of you to warn you off."

That meant Jennifer could have been responsible for the little boy's father's death AND the death of the four helpless victims strung up by their ankles.

"It was a warning to you, and to ALL of us who were on-station for your wedding. The serial killer knows you and knows about us too. You caught the attention of the killers because of who you are and what you're capable of doing to stop them. They don't want to be stopped, so they framed you so you'd be arrested. Then, when you escaped, they strung the bodies in front of you to scare you off. It's not something you're doing. It's something you've done. The killers know you'll try to stop them just liked you've stopped lawbreakers in the past. You have this righteous moral compass, Jennifer. That compass saved a little boy. That same compass helped a woman escape from jail and gave Dimitri permission to save an injured woman lying in the street. The killers know that about you and want you out of the way. "

Jennifer pictured the first oddity that started this entire sequence of events: *A blur of movement to my left jabbed my peripheral vision. As soon as it happened, it darted back into the jostling crowd like mist shot from a gun. The laser blade was on the deck in front of me, then it wasn't.*

THREE

Jennifer's mind was reeling after going back to see Russell for a second time. She had left Medico after her first exam, but on the way back to clean up in her old cabin aboard *Viper II*, she did an about-face. She returned to Medico, went in, closed the hatch, and told Russell that she had more concussion symptoms than she had admitted during her first visit.

She had bad headaches and sensitivity to light too.

As hard as its was for Jennifer to admit she needed help, it was even harder to tell Russell after promising to listen. He shrugged it off, changed her meds, and sent her on her way. That hurt too—he was such a good friend he didn't even berate her.

Jennifer now sat at the small comp desk in her cabin. The more she watched her hands, the more she realized they were trembling. The commo on the comp beeped.

"Yes," she hit the accept key and shot her hands into her lap.

"Our guest just got cleaned up and is going to meet us in the galley," Ian said.

"Be right there." She cut the feed.

Jennifer had already cleaned up, put on her civvies, brushed her hair, and taken a few pills. From what Russell said, it would take a while to get used to the medication's side effects. It had only been 15 minutes and she could already feel an airy, lightheadedness that pulled the hard tension she'd been living with for months from her head. The light in the cabin didn't bother her as much either.

Out through the hatch fast, Jennifer bumped into Spinner Babe. The woman was heading down the corridor to meet up with Ian in the galley too. The woman cradled Jennifer's hip with outstretched hands to avoid an impact.

"Whoa!"

Jennifer noticed the woman didn't release her grip at first.

"You okay now?" She looked up into Jennifer's eyes. Her hands drifted off her waist.

Jennifer knew what she meant. "Actually, no." She scanned both directions of the corridor.

"How bad is it?" Her brown eyes held concern and something else Jennifer decided to test for validity.

"I don't want you to say anything about what happened." Jennifer swallowed, baring open her trust that this woman could be counted on to keep her medical info secret.

"You shittin' me?" The gleam in the woman's eyes was playful, but there was hurt behind it too, almost as though she was insulted that Jennifer would even question such a thing.

"I, I mean—" Jennifer stammered.

"After what you did for me..." Spinner Babe scoffed. "You go first. I'll follow. Travel separate, like we didn't talk."

Jennifer smiled with relief and turned taking a step.

"Hey," the woman stopped her.

Jennifer spun around.

"Relax."

The breath Jennifer was holding rushed out. She nodded and headed for the galley.

Spinner Babe hitched her backside up on one of four galley tables. Jennifer and Ian stood in front of her. Jennifer rubbed her sore stomach by reflex.

"I apologize for smacking you in the gut so many times... didn't know Frog Face planted one on you."

"Accepted. Froggy had some skill, who'd a thought? Mind if I ask what you were in for?"

Spinner Babe stood up, extended a friendly hand, and they shook.

"My name is Carol Bouquet. Thank you for what you did."

"You're welcome." Jennifer smiled appreciatively, and not just for the introduction.

"My ex tried to force his way back into my life, and between my legs, without consent. I beat the shit out of him. Don't let my incarceration fool you though; I'd do it all over again and rot in that cell. He's going to have a very difficult time throwing more pipe even when the swelling dies down."

Ian swallowed a snicker. "I'm Ian McKivey."

"Nice to meet you, Ian. Your big body felt good against my back with shit flyin' everywhere during the riot. Thanks for giving yourself up. I mean it. I can handle myself, but if Jennifer and I had been trapped in that nook much longer no tellin' how our day would have ended." Carol looked at Jennifer. "Where's your other friend? I'd like to thank him too." She referred to Dimitri.

"Dimitri is never far away when I'm around."

Carol's brows inched up. "You two sweet on each other then?"

"You misunderstand, Carol. Dimitri is my Pinaten vassal. Do you know anything about the planet Pinat and their kinship lineage bonds?"

"I know that Pinatens can fight better than any race I've ever seen. Is that what you mean?"

"Not really, although what you said is 100 percent true. Pinaten men are part of a warrior caste society that swear felty to their liege lord as a form of honor bound devotion. Anyway, Dimitri and I are *locked at the hip* for lack of a better term. He swore fealty to me many years ago."

"I've never been to Pinat, so I didn't know that. Whatever the motivation, Dimitri has quick hands." She flipped a look at Ian. "Doesn't he?"

"He does," Ian agreed. "I didn't doubt for one-second that he'd protect Jennifer and I. He stopped that pipe from smacking my head during the riot. The cover he provided helped get us all out of there in a timely fashion."

"Timely is an understatement," Carol reiterated. "That mob shifted their attention on the unfortunate guys strung up by their ankles up over the other side of the street. After that, they looked like they were going to take their frustrations out on Station Security HQ."

"You blame them?" Jennifer asked.

"No, not really. The serial killer that's been murdering people for the last few weeks has everyone on-station terrified about who might be next. Something like this was bound to happen. I don't believe the folks from Station Security have done a bad job investigating. It's just the strange nature of the killings if you ask me."

"You think the killings are targeted?"

"Not targeted, but categorized."

"Categorized?"

Carol scooted off the table, pulled out a chair, and sat down. She was about forty years old, with hair done up in a short pixie bob cut with a sandy blonde crown. The dark brown smooth shave on the sides was undercut. The style topped her five-foot-three tiny frame like the surprise she was. It was as though her choice of hairstyle revealed her inner-self.

"Look, none of the murders are similar. Every time a person's been killed—the location, what they were doing, who they were with, all of that has been different. Only one person was alone out of eleven. Does that sound to you like a strategy for NOT getting caught? I mean, how can whoever is responsible plan the crimes, commit them, and never leave any clues? It creeps me out big time. I'm telling you the truth, Trustwords here—I'm damn glad to be off that station right now."

"The victims aren't linked. I know that because my fiancé runs the station." Jennifer took a seat across from Carol.

"Really? Ser Bantor is your fiancé?"

Jennifer groaned then looked up at Ian.

"They were supposed to get married tomorrow, Carol. Bad timing..." Ian trailed off swallowing back any more on the subject.

"Why were you arrested?" Carol asked.

"Murder and attempted kidnapping."

"I didn't know that. How were you framed?" The calm certainty of Carol's question was awesome.

"Thank you, Carol. That really feels good to hear."

"The frame had to be clever. It was, wasn't it?"

"I was removed from some equation during the riot. I was on-station cleaning up a few details early this morning with vendors providing stuff for my wedding. I was stupid not to head back to Krachy's apartment as soon as the riot started. The riot began at the Crossings and was far away at the time. I came out of a shop and saw the mob coming my way. Then a little boy and his dad were being tossed around. The next thing I knew I pulled the kid out of the way of a laser blade flying through the air."

"And you were arrested for that?"

Jennifer shook her head.

"No, the boy's father was killed by the blade. Then the damn thing ended up in my hand. All I know is that I was thrilled I saved the little boy...I still am."

"There's more, huh?"

"How do you know that, Carol?"

Carol snorted.

"There's always more with people like you. No one said you have to like this. I get that, I do. But no one said you have take responsibility for it either. Maybe what you need more than anything is a *stationer*."

"I need a what?"

"You're a target of something here, Jennifer. My guess is that with all the resources, skillsets, whatever, you have access to, the killer wants you and ALL of that out of the way. I've lived on Biltmire Station my whole life. I'm a stationer that knows the place...knows the place well." The corners of Carol's mouth lifted. "I grew up there..."

"You're a crafty little shit storm aren't you, Bouquet." Jennifer's grin matched hers.

"I am."

"All right," Jennifer came to a decision. "What do you have in mind?"

Carol shook her head. She looked up at Ian. "She always like this?"

Ian's head bobbed nodding out the answer. "Pretty much."

Jennifer's eyes moved from Carol to Ian and back. "What'd I do?"

"The correct question is: What'd you do *again*?"

Ian answered, "Full frontal, full frontal assault mode, Jennifer. That's what you're doing again."

Jennifer leaned back in her chair, blew out a breath, and rubbed her stomach.

Carol's eyes softened. "Don't start second guessing yourself. How about this—when we need to blow something up, Ian and I will break the glass on your cage and call in your air strike." She smirked.

"I can see working with you is going to be a hard lesson in humility."

"You ARE trainable!" Carol mocked.

"How did you kno—?"

"—I met Sami and we had a little chat."

Ian's look turned thoughtful. "You being framed for murder and attempted kidnapping could be as simple as someone using a sneak suit, Jennifer," he concluded.

Jennifer looked over at Carol to explain.

"Carol, what he's talking about is a stealth suit I've used before for recon work, insertions, stuff like that. The suit is a full-body plasma display that projects the background a person is in front of on its surface. In essence, it makes the person invisible. The technology is very advanced."

"Really? This isn't something you pick up at the corner store, is it?"

Jennifer replied, "No, but they are available to people that can afford them. There have been several iterations of the suits since I first started using them years ago."

"This isn't what happened this morning, was it, Jennifer?" Ian knew Jennifer would have jumped on board with the sneak suit solution if she thought that was the answer.

"No, that's not what I remember, what I think I saw."

"What did you see?" Carol asked.

"Movement, movement that was blurred but visible. I know how the sneak suits work. They're totally transparent. Completely invisible, I know this for a fact, Carol. I've taken down the most dangerous man I've ever known with a sneak suit. No, what I sensed this morning was something else. Almost, like it had to do with speed."

Ian frowned. "Speed?"

"Yes, Ian. Speed."

"Then how does speed connect to the categorization of the killings I mentioned?" Carol asked.

"I don't know how, Carol."

***

Krachy had made the decision which love demanded, the love that the woman who had chosen him deserved, the love that began the first time he met her, and which told Krachalavito Bantor that there were things you must do, regardless of your personal welfare.

So his position as Biltmire Space Station Director was ending.

"You've got to stay with this longer," Marco Sigretti said via tight beam vid trans from his heavy battle cruiser *Baneful*.

Marco Sigretti was a sturdy forty-something with black hair and watchful, patient brown eyes. Jennifer had stowed away on his ship escaping an arranged marriage on Markem when she was just 19 years old. Marco took Jennifer under his wing and gave her the first job she'd ever had on a starship once he discovered what she'd done. They'd remained friends and worked together ever since.

"I can't do that, Marco. I'm backed into a corner. I'm engaged to a person charged with murder and attempted kidnapping. Also, what's happened on-station is a direct reflection on me. Ultimately, the murders and capture of the serial killer are my responsibility. The four recent decapitations are just another example of how I've let down all the people on-station. Not to mention the people killed or injured in the riot that are still recovering in a Medico that's busting at the seams."

"Jennifer would want you to ride this out." Marco's voice was wavering now.

"I decided to protect her. The head of Sta Sec ask me to tell him where she is and I refused. I can't give her up to save my job."

"We both know Jennifer didn't do what she's been charged with, Krachy."

"It's just a job." Krachy's mouth turned up in a crooked grin.

"Did you ever think I may be more effective helping her as a member of her team? You know, doing some of the heavy lifting?"

"You think you have to repay her for what happened last year?" Marco was egging Krachy on. He knew damn well Jennifer didn't expect that.

"She took that brutal clip to the head when I was kidnapped last year. Even in the condition she was in, she still managed to keep it together long enough to organize a rescue to pull me off that hunting resort."

"I'll be interrogated next."

"I know. It'll be either you or Rand. Sta Sec just started at the top with me. They're still trying to regroup after the riot died down overnight. If not for the riot, they would have already talked to you both," Krachy concluded referring to Basley Space Operations Commander Rand Fullrider. During the mission last year Jennifer organized to rescue Krachy from a resort that was hunting humans and aliens for sport. Rand provided men and equipment.

"My team and I are already here for your wedding. Rand is docked a slip over." Marco's eyes were devious.

"See what I mean about doing damage? By the way, I'm sorry to hear about Donina's uncle dying. I know she wanted to be at the wedding if we ever have one."

"Adrianna is with Donina too." Marco said, referring to Donina Draper who was his girlfriend. Adrianna was taking leave to help Donina. She was a member of Marco's engineering team.

Marco's look was circumspect. "Didn't Jennifer help a woman escape from detention with her?"

"Yes. It may be a good idea for me to look into the background of that woman. If Jennifer helped her escape, the woman is going to be grateful for Jennifer's help."

"Grateful and willing…"

"You mean willing to assist Jennifer?"

"Yes."

Krachy bit down on his bottom lip. "I'll get back to you on what I find out about the woman that escaped with Jennifer."

"All right. I know everything's not going to get solved today. I've got a feeling the little push Jennifer received yesterday may be the break the investigation needs."

"How?"

Marco grunted. "Jennifer's going to be pissed she's been framed."

"You've got a point. Russ Sauchen has already looked her over on her ship. We can assume that. He's told her that same thing I would. I've tried to tell Jennifer to jump off the missile launcher she always rides into battles like these. But because I live with her, I can only suggest so much."

"I can't imagine someone trying to tell her what to do."

"You're not giving her enough credit. She's been a good girl for the last eight months. Yesterday wasn't her fault. She saved a little boy's life. I'm proud of her for that."

"You don't have to defend her from me."

"I know. I'm just strung tight from all the shit that's happening."

"Don't clip the string you're wrapped in, Krachy. This is just getting started."

FOUR

Food Theory Commodity Station was the Basley Star System's largest contract food producer and located within an easy shuttle flight to Biltmire Space Station. The station staffed 110 workers across three floors. This mega kitchen made enough food to feed almost 40,000 people a day and has served over 215 million meals since being built 17 years ago. This was something that Food Theory's director, Pendleton Mack, was very proud of, but he doesn't take all the credit for this accomplishment. He has a driven team of chefs, managers, and staff that make it possible.

One of those chefs was Carol Bouquet. She was Second Floor Head Chef on Food Theory. Carol worked a two-week on, two-week off shift rotation. Her schedule resembled that of a mining base worker. There were many deep space asteroid mines scattered throughout the Basley Star System and all of them rotated shifts. Carol would board a transport shuttle, work and live on Food Theory for two weeks, then return to Biltmire Station for two weeks time off.

Carol was five days into her two-week-off rotation on Biltmire Space Station when she was arrested for throttling her ex-husband and thrown in detention. When Jennifer Bane crashed into her life, Carol had been incarcerated for two days. Now she was back on Food Theory armed with a side-door plan of action to help identify the criminal organization responsible for the serial killings on Biltmire, and ultimately, how and why Jennifer Bane was framed for attempted kidnapping and murder.

Carol had hit it off with Sami when they met back on *Viper II* and asked Sami if she wanted to help her with her plan. Sami volunteered straightaway.

Sami's forehead creased. "Why do I feel like I'm high up?"

"We're starting on the top floor where all the food comes in by cargo ship then is cleaned, cut and prepped," Carol explained waving an arm at the open loading dock blast hatches where workers were guiding anti-grav pallets of fresh food into the top floor kitchen.

"Every day workers prepare the following day's raw ingredients. The prepped food is stored in a cold room that can hold up to three tons of food. Each day the meals we prepare use the food that has been prepped the day before."

Sami turned watching workers unload anti-grav food pallets down the two cargo ship ramps.

Carol continued, "On an average day we use about 25 different ingredients in this three-floor mega kitchen." Sami followed Carol toward a lift tube in the corner of the large docking bay. As they walked, Sami turned right looking out into the black, star-twinkling depths of deep space behind the two cargo ships. The magnetic containment field held back the deadly vacuum beyond. The two women had just disembarked from one of the two cargo ships.

Sami shot a hand out grabbing Carol's forearm before Carol hit the lift tube call button.

"Are you sure you aren't worried that Food Theory knows all about your ongoing incarceration?"

Carol chuckled. "Hell no! Food Theory isn't affiliated with Biltmire. This is a privately owned commodity station. Besides, no one gives me any static around here. You'll see." The corner of her mouth quirked up.

Inside the synth glass transparent lift tube, the two women could see the different levels of the mega kitchen stream by on their way down to the first floor. Because the station was preparing such a large quantity of food very quickly, and very cost efficiently, they used a lot of high-tech machines. Automated sorting and cutting machines were being manned by workers. There were even servo droids rolling to different locations to perform repetitive tasks. Once the top floor finished prepping the veggies, grains, meat, and fish, the food was funneled down through shoots that connected to the second floor. This simple use of gravity was one of the key components of the facility as it reduced the amount of manual labor and kept things clean.

On the second floor, the different ingredients landed in one of 25 stainless steel cauldrons where robotic arms used large stirrers to mix everything together. Steam cooked the food in the massive cauldrons then it was dropped down through shoots to the first floor.

Sami and Carol exited the lift tube on the first floor and paused.

"Once the food drops down here," Carol swung an arm toward the large room talking loudly over the noise of all the packaging equipment, "it gets portioned and packed into individual vessels for distribution."

The two women turned and made their way through a hatch. On the other side of the hatch, the loud noise of the packaging floor faded.

"Over there," Carol pointed.

They strode past a hatch with *Administration* stenciled on it, past a hatch labeled *Staff Accommodations*, then finally in through the *Ward Room* hatch.

The guy behind the bar in the lounge section of the large ward room straitened when Carol approached the bar. The young man's eyes darted back-and-forth between the two women. His throat seemed to tighten as he spoke.

"Get you something, Ms. Bouquet?"

"Two beers. Be quick about it," she barked.

The guy hurried to fill the order, and was back fast, dropping two mugs on the bar.

Carol grabbed the mugs, tilted her head toward a booth, and Sami followed her over as they scrunched in on either side of the table. Since it wasn't shift change, the place wasn't very busy. Carol pushed one of the mugs over to Sami and smiled smugly.

"Most of the people on-station are scared shitless of me. I'm head chef on the second floor and run the floor like a tyrant. They even have a nickname for me."

"What's that?" Sami asked.

"Bastard Chef."

Sami snickered and clinked Carol's mug as they both took a pull on their beers.

"Sami, you were telling me Jennifer let you and her team do most of the work on your last mission. Working on a mission like this is all kinda new to me, but I got the sense that Jennifer was hesitant to let you and I try to get things rolling by starting this mission on Food Theory. I had the distinct impression that Jennifer was worried about getting me more involved than I already am."

"I'm sure she was," Sami pushed a strand of dark brown hair behind an ear. She was in a similar pair of gray cargo trousers like Carol but had on a dark blue knit long sleeve shirt that outlined her thin physique. She was only 26 years old but finely attractive. Her eyes blazed with something Carol couldn't quite place.

"Jennifer's always concerned about her friends. Her crew too. She figures you're a part of that now."

Carol studied Sami. "I know you and her have a history, a lot of which is none of my business. I saw this mission as an opportunity to give something back. You know, to Biltmire and my friends who live there. You understand?"

"More than you know, Carol."

"So, after Ian and I finally convinced Jennifer that a side-door plan starting here on Food Theory was better than a full frontal assault, they both agreed my idea might work. What do you think?"

"Pretty solid," Sami's eyes sparkled. "No one would anticipate being able to pinpoint the location of the group responsible for the killings on Biltmire the way you suggested. I would have never thought of it."

"I guess you just have to do what I do all the time. Food is the life blood of any space station. The process for preparing individual portions and delivering the food once its packaged is very complex. The complexity of that process blew my mind when I first started learning about it. That's one of the reasons I don't manage first floor packaging operations. Too damn complicated for me. I like being the head chef on the second floor, much less complex."

"But just the thing we need to help find out who's doing the serial killings on Biltmire, right?"

"I think so. There are many kinds of food we deliver to Biltmire. There are also a number of tiers."

"Tiers, what do you mean?"

"Like any food supplier, we have grades of quality. Three to be exact: eco, mid and top."

"How does that help find the group of people responsible for the serial killings?"

"I don't necessarily think it does. Because, for example, an apartment block on-station may give us an order for two tiers of food they serve to residents in their mess hall. They may offer some low end, eco tier food to residents. The apartment block may also offer some higher end, mid tier, for their residents to eat too. The key to my plan for finding out who the serial killers are is the destination and quantity of food that is delivered to a customer, not the tiers. You and I are going to use the destination and quantity information to track the food to its final customer. We are going to attempt to use destination and quantity data to locate the criminal group responsible for the killings."

"How will that help us find this group?"

"To start with, process of elimination, Sami. I can log into Food Theory's distribution computer. Once in, I can eliminate all the legit customers we deliver to. I can probably eliminate over 80 or 90 percent of the end customers as legitimate or not just by looking at their order history."

Sami raised a brow. "I get it. The group that's been doing all the killing has only been operating for a short period of time, right?"

"Partly, yes, but the two most important things that are going to make or break my plan are quantity and concentration. First, the quantity of food that this secret organization orders can't be very large. Second, for this to be a good way to track where the organization is, they have to eat together in one place, concentrated."

"Concentrated?"

"Yes," Carol took a drink. "If this small criminal group is spread out and doesn't eat their meals together in one place, then what I'm proposing may just be a waste of time."

"It won't be waste of time, Carol." Sami swallowed a gulp.

"If this group is not eating together at meal times my plan is shit. The destination of the food won't be delivered to just one place. If not, we may not find them. So yeah, this could be a waste of time."

"No, it won't be. I have enough experience to tell you that missions like these are very fluid. If we go down one rat hole, it will only open up another one for us to consider."

"You're giving me more credit than I think I deserve."

Sami's jaw clinched, like she refused to believe that failure was an option. "At least we'll be back on-station, regardless."

"What?"

Sami perched her elbows on the table cupping her mug. She glanced around the ward room then looked at Carol.

"Your plan is going to get us back on Biltmire Station. We can't find out who's doing the killings way out here. We can't just take a transport shuttle to Biltmire. Everyone that comes on-station has to go through security screening. You're a wanted fugitive, Carol. You just escaped from detention. There's no way Biltmire Sta Sec would ever guess that you'd come back on-station in a food transport. Food transports aren't screened."

"You'll have to handle the food deliveries, Sami."

"That shouldn't be a problem for me. I'm not wanted for escaping detention. I have free run of the station. I can scout out every customer that takes delivery of their food. I'm smart enough to know which ones look legit and which ones don't. Even if I can't tell right away, I can feed the info back to you and you can do your own recon for a closer look. The best part is that I'm going to have help once I'm on-station."

"Sure you will, Food Theory guarantees delivery of every order. There'll be several other delivery staff from Food Theory helping you. I have enough pull to get you slotted in on the food transport as one of the delivery staff."

"No, Carol, that's not what I mean. I'll have on-station help from Jennifer's wedding party. There are two ships docked on Biltmire filled with Jennifer's friends that are there to attend her wedding." Sami's eyes glinted.

Carol was slow on the uptake, then her brows knitted.

"Jennifer's friends are not just your run-of-the-mill civilians are they?"

"Of course not," Sami leaned back, took a pull of beer and gave Carol a half-smile.

"You want me to list some of skills these people have or are you putting the pieces together now?"

"If even one of Jennifer's friends is as good as that Dimitri guy from Pinat, you'll have all the help you need."

Sami's face beamed.

"What?"

"Well, I don't think *anyone* is as awesome as Dimitri, but I may be a little biased..."

"Huh?"

"He's my Pinaten man hunk, Carol."

"Your what?"

Sami's eyebrows waggled.

Carol studied her. "He's your husband isn't he?"

"Not husband, but close enough."

"You know he pretty much saved our asses during the riot, don't you? I never did get to chance to thank him for that."

"Dimitri knows you appreciate what he did. I thanked him for you."

"Nice," Carol smiled.

"How does Food Theory handle specialty restaurants on Biltmire? You know, eateries that cook made-to-order food people can order off a menu."

"Restaurants on Biltmire place their orders directly with us. The third floor preps what the restaurants order. Then the fresh food bypasses being cooked on the second floor and is fed down shoots directly to the first floor packaging operation. The food is portioned and put in vessels then loaded on a cargo ship and sent on its way. Orders for fresh products are tracked on Food Theory's distribution computer. I can look at order histories and see which of the restaurants are legit and how long the restaurant has been ordering with us. So when you deliver food once you're on-station, you'll be delivering fresh product to restaurants too." Carol threw back a last gulp of beer. She dug in her pocket and pulled out a hand comp. "I'm going to get your on-boarding as a food delivery worker started."

Sami drank the last of her beer watching Carol's fingers peck out commands on the hand comp.

Carol looked up. "Since you're not in the shit house with Biltmire like me, we can use your real name. What's your last name?"

"Bane."

Recognition dawned on Carol's face.

Before she could ask, Sami said, "No, not her sister, not by blood anyway," she smiled faintly. "Long story…"

Carol shrugged an arm but kept on tapping in commands.

"That does it. I have some discretionary funds I can use as part of my second floor budget. The best plan is to just go ahead and add you as a temp worker. That way we can swing by Administration and pick up an ID and uniform for you before we leave. Let's go."

The two women sprung up and headed for the exit. Out in the corridor they made a right into Administration and within five minutes Sami had a badge and a uniform strung over a finger on a clothes hanger. The women exited Admin out into the corridor.

Carol explained as they walked toward the packaging room, "Packaged food gets loaded into waiting cargo ships docked on the other side of the packaging room here on the first floor." They entered the leftmost hatch into the loud packaging room. Carol turned extending a hand motioning Sami to hold up. "It's an all hands type of operation." She bellowed over the noise.

"What is?" Sami shouted.

"Loading food into the cargo ships." Carol jerked her head toward the woman's WC. "Duck in there and change into your uniform. You and I are going to help tie down the food pallets in the cargo hold on one of the transports. Wait for me at the blast hatch over there," she pointed then turned back to Sami. "But don't, I repeat *don't*, go through. Wait for me to come and get you."

Sami nodded, turned and headed for the woman's WC.

When Sami was done putting on the uniform, Carol came back into the packaging room and motioned for Sami to follow her through the blast hatch into the loading dock. The loading dock operation was a dangerous place to be, especially for Sami. Carol grabbed Sami's arm yanking her back a step. A rolling servo droid guiding an enormous anti-grav pallet of food vessels moved past oblivious to any human, or anything else, in its way.

"It's orchestrated chaos," Carol let go of Sami's arm. "You and I do the tie downs in the cargo hold of a cargo ship that is heading to Biltmire. While you were changing I arranged for us to tie down the hot food pallets. The automated equipment will guide the food pallets up into the cargo ship hold. When an anti-grav pallet is moving close to its final tie down location, it slows automatically, then we use verbal commands to make any slight adjustments to secure the pallet in the hold."

"What commands?"

"Stop, slow forward, slow left, slow right, those are the only commands we need."

Sami nodded and waited for Carol to lead the way. At first Sami didn't know why Carol was not moving toward the cargo ship ramp. She was about to ask when another large pallet entered through one of the large blast hatches to her right fast. Sami could feel the wind across her face as the huge, dangerous, servo-droid-manned anti-grav pallet whizzed by. Carol fell in jogging behind the waist-high servo droid guiding the large pallet. Up the ramp it went and a man in the fore section of the cargo hold yelled stop. Carol anticipated the command and had already slowed to a stop herself. Sami didn't and accidentally barreled into Carol's back with outstretched arms to stop her momentum.

The man in front of the pallet walked around it, handed the hammer he was holding to Carol, and nodded.

"All yours Ms. B, thanks for the help." The man smiled and stopped at the bottom of the ramp then jogged to the exit blast hatch once his path was safe.

Carol explained, "I told him I'd take his shift but that he'd still get paid for it." She smirked. "He loved that!"

"Bet he did," Sami agreed. "You may not the Bastard Chef they say you are."

Carol walked purposefully past the pallet while talking.

"I raise hell when people screw up, but when they kick ass, I'm the first one to compliment them for a job well done." She stopped and turned to face Sami. "Everyone knows I'm hard but fair. Move behind me and watch what I do." Carol hooked an arm around Sami's waist pulling her behind her. "Slow forward," she instructed.

The huge pallet inched toward her. "Slow left," she instructed and the pallet inched its way to both Carol and Sami's right. Sami understood what the computer-driven pallet was doing. The point of reference for the computer-guided servo droid was *loading ramp in.*

"Slow forward...stop!" The pallet moved toward them then stopped. Auto hooks in each of the four corners of the pallet extruded from the cargo ship deck and inserted into the female receptacles with a loud snap. Carol looked at Sami.

"You have to manually check each tie-down hook. The machines are good, but a visual verify has to be done or a pallet could shift during transport. That spells disaster," she bent down. "Look here, Sami." She motioned for Sami to get down on a knee next to her. "We use a hammer and smack the shit out it." Carol raised the large hammer in her hand, wound up and clanked the tie-down hook. It sounded like a dull thud, barely an echo in the confines of the cargo hold. She locked eyes with Sami. "The sound is the key. If it's a dull thud like that, it's good to go, totally secure."

Sami nodded, and Carol handed her the hammer. "I'll guide the next pallet in while you check the other three corners on this one."

Sami did as she was told, three dull thuds later, and the next pallet inched its way into an open tie-down slot right behind the pallet Sami just checked.

It took less than 20 minutes to finish tying down the last of the hot food pallets in the cargo ship hold. Sami noticed that Carol didn't recheck any of her tie-hook smacks to ensure she'd not made a mistake. The two woman made their way out of the cargo hold into the tight confines of the crew ward room on the cargo ship. Several other workers were in the ward room gripping anything they could find bracing themselves for take off. The fully laden cargo ship took off and slowly surged away from Food Theory picking up speed. The flight to Biltmire would take about two hours.

"Not dead-heading this time, Ms. B?" One of the three other delivery food workers seated at the far end of the ward room table asked Carol.

Carol shook her head.

"No, not hitching a free ride back on-station this time, Najee," she told the middle-aged dark skinned man. "Today is Sami's first day delivering food. I wanted to make sure she doesn't screw up. If she does a good job, I'll think about transitioning her to full-time. You guys are going to look after her today, aren't you?" The question was no question at all. The delivery workers knew who Carol was.

Three heads nodded, then the workers continued their low-key conversation.

Carol turned to Sami.

"We have some time, so I'm going to login to the distribution comp and start checking the quantity and destination of all the cargo back in the hold." Head down, Carol started her research.

Sami watched her and thought of something.

"We won't have to worry about the largest vessels of food being delivered to legit customers, right?"

"Right, look here." Carol turned the hand comp screen toward Sami and pointed.

"There are a total of 18 pallets in the hold. Twelve are *just-in-time* hot food deliveries that will be consumed within an hour of being off loaded on-station. Only two of the hot food pallets are going to be broken down into smaller orders that will be delivered to individual customers." She pulled the hand comp back tapping the screen.

"Turn on your synch mate so I can send you a run sheet for the hot food deliveries you're going to deliver today," Carol instructed, referring to the terminology delivery workers used to route plan their deliveries once on-station.

Sami's hand comp pinged. She studied the small screen.

Carol said, "You're going to deliver hot just-in-time con-sumables. Here's my thinking— The customers taking delivery will be eating the hot food as soon as they get it. That will give you an opportunity to see the group of people that are going to eat the food because they will be eating their meal together." Carol lifted an eyebrow.

"Concentrated, right?"

Carol's mouth twisted. "It's kinda thin, I know, but yes. You may get lucky and spot a group of people that look suspicious, or downright evil, while they're gathered waiting for their food to arrive. If the hair on the back of your neck stands up, we may get lucky right away. If you see a group of people that set off your radar these *Hair Raisers* might be the serial killers we're looking for…maybe. "

"If not, it goes back to what you said—process of elimination."

"Basically, yes, this is just a hard target search with the best information we have. But it's a start. You agree?"

"I agree." Sami gave Carol a once-over.

"What?"

"I don't want you to be surprised if a member of Jennifer's team contacts you. Whether you stay on board the cargo ship or wait in the landing bay, there's a chance one of her team will get in touch with you once we arrive on-station."

Carol scrutinized Sami's face finding what she was looking for.

"They'll know who I am. They'll probably know all about me, won't they?"

"Without a doubt, Carol. Jennifer's team is not going to blow your cover, but they will try to help us."

"So, do you need to contact them to tell them we're headed to Biltmire?"

Sami shook her head. "No need."

FIVE

Sami and Carol portioned out the hot food vessels that were denoted on Sami's run sheet and placed them into a large smart cart cargo vehicle. The smart cart, complete with human-like precision, had a full range of mobility and speed. It was a tall, four-foot-wide, circle-shaped rolling cargo container. The cart could crawl to stay in pace with Sami or even dash along in a sprint. It auto-followed a few paces behind her as she strode down the cargo ramp and out through the landing bay blast hatch to make her deliveries. In addition to expedited travel, the cart allowed Sami to be hands-free so she could consult the run sheet on her hand comp planning each delivery stop.

Carol watched Sami and the smart cart exit through the blast hatch when the hand comp in her pocket vibrated. A shot of adrenaline knifed her chest as she slapped a hand over it by reflex. It kept vibrating. She turned and made her way back into the now empty ward room on-board the cargo ship.

She pulled the hand comp to her ear hesitantly.

"Hola, Señorita Bouquet," the woman's voice said.

"Hello?"

"We have a mutual friend that has a problem. Let's not say her name." The woman spoke slowly and precisely to make certain Carol understood.

There was a pause while Carol took that in. She hadn't expected to be contacted by someone on Jennifer's team so quickly.

"Yes, yes that's right. She talked to you?"

"Of course, Ms. B. I'm prepared to help with the problem. I know you don't know me, but I hope our mutual friend's help with your liberation will be the evidence that you can trust me."

The women even knew that one of Carol's nicknames was "Ms. B" and that she escaped from detention, *how the...?*

"Don't feel threatened, Bastard Chef. You and I are gonna meet. Can you make your stealthy little way to The Freak Fam Rave tonight?"

How the heck this woman knew the name of the under-deck club scene on-station was a mystery. The Freak Family was the name of Carol's underground rave click she was a part of. Biltmire Space Station didn't allow rave parties top-side. Raves had been outlawed two years ago when drugs and debauchery took its toll and several people overdosed on Gleam and died. Ever since then, the illegal parties went sub-terranean. In this case, under-deck. The Freak Fam held their raves covertly, in the jumbled mesh of maintenance tunnels directly beneath the living streets of Biltmire Space Station.

Making her stealthy little way to The Freak Fam Rave was routine for Carol. She had traveled the complicated paths, tunnels, ducts, and passageways under Biltmire's shiny pedestrian streets countless times. She thought back to the first few times she had used the labyrinth of maintenance and mechanical catacombs so many years ago: *Back then, I was unmoored, unattached, and excited to meet new friends in this grubby underworld free from the judging eyes of all the top-siders.* She was not unmoored now because no sooner than she divorced her husband, Jennifer Bane entered her life. Now one of Jennifer's team had contacted Carol and offered to meet her on her own turf, her own territory. Carol was now in her refuge, her domain, and it felt good. The thought occurred to Carol: *The woman that contacted me must have known this, must have known that meeting under-deck would make me feel safe.*

Carol needed to change her clothes. There was no way she could go by her apartment top-side to get some; she was a wanted fugitive. She was still in her civvies, and that wasn't comfortable. The heat moving through the pipes, conduits, and ducts under-deck was extreme in some places and generally uncomfortable in others. Carol also wanted to be free. Under-deck was her second home, where she could always be herself, her true inner-self.

Carol slowed as the person up ahead came into view in the dark tunnel.

"You got pinched, Carol. Yet, here you are…"

The dark haired man reached out in traditional Freak Fam greeting. He rested a hand on Carol's shoulder, caressed her bicep, forearm, then ran his hand up to her neck, gripping her thin throat lightly before releasing it. He smiled.

"You need better garb, babe." His eyes scanned her clothes.

This was what Carol loved about her family—no questions, no judgement, only acceptance. It felt good to be back under-deck, but the heat around her was pulling sweat from every pore on her body.

"Where's Lan? She should have good garb." Carol returned the Freak Fam greeting, careful to take her time as a show of mutual respect. Every member of the FF was important and interconnected. Her instincts kicked in, her inner chrono slowing, to adjust itself to under-deck time.

The man glanced down the utilidor, which was a utility tunnel passage that carried utility lines such as electricity, steam, water supply pipes, and even sewer pipes. The heat along with the smell was unmistakable.

"Down, left one, you'll see her." He motioned with a hand down the dim lit corridor.

"Thanks."

Carol smiled, wiped her sleeve across her face a few times pulling some sweat away, then turned down the utilidor. At the T junction, the faint bass of electro-dance music was more pronounced. Carol took the left and up ahead were two dark figures shrouded in steam mist hugging one side of the narrow rectangular tunnel.

The women on the left smiled as Carol approached.

"Hi, Lan," Carol smiled back.

Lan had on some sheer lingerie and bowed at the waist, then straightened, locking eyes with Carol. Both women performed greeting. Done greeting, Lan was handed some skimpy clothing from the other woman Carol did not recognize. Carol extended an arm to take the clothes then the new-face brushed past Lan, dropped the clothes, and performed the FF greeting as though she had done it a thousand times. Carol's apprehension about new-face melted in the ritual.

"My name is Murphy, Carol." Her smile lingered in true FF connect then she used some common slang that denoted honesty. "Trustwords—I'm here to help Jennifer. And to deliver a thank you from her for what you are doing."

Murphy was a hacker by trade and a genius by birth. She had been instrumental in helping rescue Krachy off the hunting resort eight months ago. Murphy was on-station now as part of Jennifer's wedding party and jumped at the chance to work with Carol. Besides, Sami said Carol was an under-decker. Murphy had heard about the Freak Fam on Biltmire and wasn't going to miss her chance to be a part of it.

Relaxed now, Carol shed her clothes without hesitation. Naked, she wiped her gray shirt up and down both arms and legs, crotch, underarms, and face. She picked up the two black fishnet nylons off the deck and scrunched them on over each leg to her upper thigh. She picked up the eyelash-lace sheer black teddy, then pulled it up and slipped both arms through. The front covered each A cup breast with a wide gap down the center to show off her sternum tattoo. The tattoo was a thin, black upside down squiggly circle thinning to a point between Carol's small breasts.

Murphy eyed her. "Better?"

Carol let out a long breath. "Much!" She picked up the stilettos then looked over at Lan.

"Lan, I'm going to have words with Murphy." Lan nodded. "Thank you for the garb."

Lan smiled as Carol and Murphy walked back to the T junction, took the right, then stopped. The electro vibes were still thumping but not a hinderance while they spoke.

"You called me earlier on my hand comp." Carol extended an arm steadying herself against the corridor wall as she slipped one three-inch stack stiletto on then the other.

"I did."

"Any word from Sami?"

"Yes. You up for scoping out three possibles?"

Carol shook her head. "I should have known. Well, if we're going to run down leads, I can't very well do it in these." She bent over and pulled off the stilettos. "Gimme a sec." She walked around the corner and was back fast, wearing the two civvy shoes she'd taken off earlier.

Carol dipped her eyes to Murphy's feet.

"You were ready for this," she said, noticing Murphy already had on comfortable looking flats.

Murphy nodded. She had on a black mesh bodycon dress over bra and panties complementing her jet black short hair. The stretch mesh long sleeves covered her arm tattoos, but the scoop neck revealed swirling artwork on her chest that crept up her neck. A few round cut-outs down the front and down each side exposed more creative tats of a lighter color. Carol's brows knitted noticing that Murphy was waiting for her to lead the way.

"You knew I'd be able to find a way through under-deck to the places we need to investigate, didn't you?"

"You grew up here, Carol."

"We gonna need backup or is this strictly recon?"

"Recon only. We're going to attempt to put eyes on three groups of people Sami spotted that stood out to her when she was making food deliveries. The last group made the hairs stand up on the back of her neck, just like you said it might. That group could be the Hair Raisers we're looking for. At least that's what Sami seemed to think when she saw them take delivery of their food."

Carol swallowed. Things were moving fast and she realized what Sami told her back on Food Theory was true. This mission was a fluid situation.

Murphy saw the apprehension on Carol's face.

"We can abort anytime. I don't want to come face-to-face with any psycho killers either, Carol. Trustwords." Murphy reached out a hand cupping Carol's neck reassuringly.

Carol closed her eyes, letting out a breath. She tilted her head into Murphy's hand as it inched up caressing the side of Carol's head and ear. Carol leaned her head into it more, relaxing noticeably.

Carol opened her eyes as Murphy pulled back her hand. She watched Murphy pull off two, sometimes three rings, off each finger then reach up to stash the clanking metal into a small alcove up between two pipes overhead.

"Not a good idea to advertise myself crawling down an air duct," Murphy explained referring to the rings.

Murphy pulled out her hand comp from a mesh pocket on her hip. She touched the screen pulling up the three locations then turned the display toward Carol. Carol studied it.

"The first place is the farthest away." She locked eyes with Murphy. "The least dangerous in Sami's opinion, right?"

"Yes, it'll be best to recon the Hair Raisers last. That'll give us the opportunity to bail out if we're tired, or if by some off chance, we do find something important at the first two places. Sound good?"

"Sounds good."

Murphy reached back into her mesh pocket and extracted four small button shaped devices. Holding up two of them she explained.

"Sub-vocal mic and an earbud." She pressed the sub-vocal microphone to her throat. It stayed in place. Then the earbud went into an ear. "Here," Murphy handed Carol a set.

Carol put them both in place. "Comm check, test, test," she whispered.

Murphy nodded. "Good to go," then she fingered the screen on her hand comp powering it down. "The comms work independent of my hand comp and have about 30 minutes talk time. I don't want my hand comp vibrating at the wrong time, so I turned it off. You can lead the way anytime you're ready." There was no urgency in Murphy's suggestion as she was now completely locked into under-deck time as well.

Carol had the picture of the three locations she'd looked at on Murphy's hand comp in her mind. She knew exactly where to go. All three locations would take them through the Freak Fam Rave into outlying parts of Biltmire Station far from were they were now. Carol rounded the corner taking the left, Murphy falling in behind heading toward the first recon target.

The deep house electro vibes increased in volume. The utilidor acted like a megaphone. The sound had nowhere to go in the close confines of under-deck, so the Rave DJ didn't need to turn up the volume that loud. Thirty or forty people moved rhythmically up ahead, bobbing to the repetitive beat of the music. The corridor did not widen. Raves were held where the Freak Fam gathered that night, and were always held in different locations under-deck. Little was needed to hold a rave: a hand comp, a speaker, and a DJ. Holding the raves in a different location meshed nicely with the vagabond nature of the Freak Fam. Moving locations every time also made if more difficult for Biltmire Station Security to pinpoint the raves, thus preventing Sta Sec from intervening and shutting them down.

The two woman shuffled and squeezed through the Ravers. The close body contact of the sweating, dancing, Freak Fams pulled yet more streams of sweat from Carol and Murphy. Finally past the DJ, the corridor came to a T junction and Carol turned right. The speaker pushing out the thumping house music was aimed in the opposite direction down the tunnel behind them, and after two more turns in the utilidor, the sound receded behind them.

Sami was correct. The first two groups of people Murphy and Carol put eyes on did not seem a high threat. Granted, what they were doing was illegal, but not psychotic or deadly per se. The first two groups were not the serial killers they were searching for. The first group were thieves. The activities Carol and Murphy witnessed as they inched their way through an overhead O^2 air duct, were not deadly. This group was buying stolen goods for resale at a profit. These *Fencers* were using the first location to sort and repackage the stolen goods acting as middlemen between thieves and buyers. Fencers work with thieves to buy stolen goods then resell them for a large profit.

The second group, though more sinister, were not the serial killers they were searching for either. This group was engaged in Gleam manufacture and distribution. The drug was known for its euphoric effects and was being packaged into a new delivery method. Gleam was normally taken in pill form or ground into a powder and smoked through a vape stick. This criminal group was taking Gleam and rendering the drug into a liquid for use in pre-packaged inhalers. The criminal group was expanding their market by bypassing the need for a vape stick. Instead, the pre-portioned inhalers could be used a measured number of times then disposed of.

It had taken over an hour-and-a-half of under-deck travel to recon the first two groups. Carol stopped at a vertical ladder next to a raceway system of surface mounted wire moldings. The raceway went up and acted like a channel for cables and wires. The ladder was next to the raceway to allow maintenance workers access to the entire length of the wire moldings. Cool air rushed down from the raceway above. The moving air helped evaporate some of the sweat on both women. They stood contemplating the Hair Raisers' location that needed reconnoitered last. This location made the hairs stand up on the back of Sami's neck, hence the name. The Hair Raisers could be the group of people responsible for the serial killings. The first two locations were a bust.

"I know the way, but the raceway up there's tight. It can only fit one person." Carol then jabbed a look at Murphy. "The wires and cables are electrical. No steam, or sewage, that's why it's cooler here. The Hair Raisers are up over the second floor balcony, tucked behind a retail store. I figure the retail store is their front to look legit. What's going on in the back rooms is what has Sami so worried, I would guess."

"How far should I follow behind you before stopping so I don't give your position away?"

Carol's heart was beating much too fast. The cool air moving over her chest was cold against her right nipple piercing. She looked down, pulled back the sheer fabric over her breast, and decided to take if off.

The piercing was a tiny silver internally threaded barbell. Carol gently unscrewed one ball while holding the other one. The ball came off and she pulled the shaft out through her nipple then dropped the decorative jewelry to the deck. She rubbed her breast delaying the inevitable. Her mouth was dry, and she couldn't seem to find any moisture with her tongue. Before Murphy could offer to take her place, Carol lifted her eyes, her pupils were huge.

"You don't know the correct route, Murphy. Once I leave the ladder raceway, they'll be at least eight bends in the air ducts. I used to play up there when I was a kid. At that time it was a bakery, and the smell was awesome."

"We can bail. There's no shame in it."

God this was bad—Carol didn't even know if there was a group of killers waiting up there to be discovered, but she was very scared. Knowing that she might be the first person to see who was responsible for committing such heinous acts made her tremble inside.

Determination yanked her hard around, her arms extended and she started to climb, both hands pulling her one after another up each rung. She scrunched her shoulders at the top of the utilidor as the vertical raceway narrowed. The wire moldings to her right were cool on her shoulder and hip. Her teddy caught on a jagged metal connector joining two pipes. The raceway was barely wide enough to pull herself up the ladder and bend each knee to place a foot on the next rung. Carol let the snag pull her teddy all the way off. She thought back to when Murphy pulled all her rings off and was now glad she took off her nipple piercing. She was going to be crawling naked on her belly soon, and a clanging, scratching, piece of metal on her chest would not be good.

Murphy saw her teddy get snagged and said, "Take your time, Carol. No points for speed."

It took almost 15 minutes to travel the two floors in the cramped space. At the top of the second floor she paused. Fear clawed up her throat as she thought she heard something. She decided to risk a closer look and peekèd up over the ledge above her that turned left through a narrow crawlspace. There it was again, almost like whimpering, a feeble cry.

The noise was no mistake. The faint sound echoed through the ductwork captured by her ears.

Carol didn't know what to do. She had never been afraid of anything or anybody her whole life. That was how she was raised, but in this situation she simply did not have a clue.

"Only I know you're there. No one else does, Carol." It was Murphy in her ear. A calming tone.

"You're right," Carol replied, trying to convince herself.

The loud shrill of a woman, then a clatter.

Carol scrambled up into the vent, past the top ledge, and lay flat, unmoving. The sides of the air vent rubbed her shoulders. She started sweating with fear. Pulling herself forward on the smooth metal against her chest was a challenge. The sweat on her bare skin might make a skin squeak and give her position away.

Carefully, without sound, three pulls forward, a fourth, then several more she inched her way to a vent opening on her right. Dim light spilled in through the fine grate painting the left side of the air duct. Her stomach was wet all over, and she could feel the puddle under her skin. The liquid pool cushioning her was enough to slide on. She used the gathering sweat, then pulled herself carefully forward to peek into the vent opening.

A serious looking woman was on the other side of the room sitting at a desk working knobs on a control board. The woman looked up. Carol could not see beyond the top of the grate opening. A woman's shriek of terror rose in volume from high up in the room. The woman came into Carol's view passing by the grate opening then stopping abruptly with a clank. The wind from the free fall rushed past Carol's face through the grate. The woman whimpered, consumed in a state of panic. She was bound by both wrists and each ankle face-down in a square metal fixture that had been dropped like a rock by thin metal cables attached to each corner.

The terrified woman cried out, "I can't stand the height, please don't do it again. I'll conform, I will. Don't take me up again, I beg you. Please! Please!" Stone-Face-Lady flipped a switch. "Nooo! Oh, nooo, not again!" The bound woman shot straight up out of sight, her pleading cries fading the higher she went.

Carol wished she could throw her hands to her ears, but she couldn't. The woman at the desk showed no emotion. She fingered the down-switch and the helpless captive dropped fast in the fixture. The scared women came rushing down, the metal frame jerking hard to a loud stop by the taught wires.

"Ahhhh! I can't take it again! Now my rejection hurts too. Take me down and give me the drugs. I'll conform, you saw it, I can be integrated soon. Please, let me try. Please!"

Stone-Face-Lady spoke for the first time. "It's all up to you."

The terrified woman was tiring with fear. She gulped in huge breaths trying to control her dread.

Under the cover of the woman's heavy breathing, Carol started moving again. Up ahead was a left turn. She was careful to turn on her side and push herself around the ninety degree turn at a glacial pace to avoid projecting any unwanted sound. She whispered, "Still searching." She didn't have the understanding or desire to try to explain what she'd just seen to Murphy. Carol kept moving.

The darkness of the narrow air duct she crawled in was only interrupted by murky light streaming through vent grates up ahead. As she approached another grate on her right, dread twisted in her gut. A man's muffled voice was shrill with terror, but he couldn't speak. She eased her eyes just past the corner of the grate to see. A man was tied down on an operating table.

The color drained from the middle-aged man's face which was framed by a transparent plasti helmet suctioned to the front of his head. The see-through device was rounded out away from his face several inches. At eye level, a round tube arched up in a straight line into the ceiling high above.

The man inhaled, frantic with fear, but didn't let out his breath. Carol found herself rocking her body ever so slightly back-and-forth urging the man to take a breath. Then what she saw start creeping slowly from the tube opening in the ceiling made the blood freeze in her veins.

Dozens of large hairy brown spiders began crawling down the long transparent tube toward the man's encased face. The man was mute with horror. His hands gripped the rails of his gurney so tight the veins in his arms were pulsing. His eyes were focused on the narrow tunnel of spiders creeping closer to his face. His eyes had nowhere to go but look up through the tube. His head was secured in a fixture around the chin and throat. Gravity pulled the swarming mass of spiders down through the tube faster until they were within inches of exiting to leap onto the man's face. Abruptly, a loud vacuum kicked on in the ceiling sucking the swirling host of creatures up through the tube in a blink. By then the man's eyes were clamped shut refusing to watch his inevitable fate. Eyes still shut, he finally took a breath.

A thin bald man came into view, pulled a syringe from his side, and stuck it into the terrified man's arm.

"I'm not withholding the rejection drugs, you see? I'm giving you your regular dose. Just picture what will happen when the vacuum isn't turned on next time. This is just another method to make certain you conform. There will always be a way to make you conform, *always*. I'll leave you to think that over while the rejection drugs pull your internal pain away. You can rest now." The man turned and left the room through the hatch. When the hatch shut behind him, the deadbolt clanked twice.

Carol found that she had just let out her own breath. She rolled on her side, her back against the duct behind her trying to make sense of it all. She couldn't. But what she could do was realize that now was the time to bail, leave, escape! "I'm bailing," she whispered, then gently pushed herself flat eyeing the T junction up ahead. She had an idea.

When she was certain that the bald man would not return, she pulled herself forward slowly to the T. Carol twisted left until the apex of the T was at her waist, then pulled her legs to her chest. She then extended them into the other side of the T and pushed her body backward until her chest could turn and crawl back the way she'd just come. She took what seemed like forever to get back to the ladder in the vertical raceway of wire moldings. However, that was by design. Her panic over being caught was ample motivation to move without sound.

Down the ladder Carol went; Murphy was waiting at the base of the ladder holding the ripped black teddy. She handed it to Carol.

Carol grabbed the lingerie. She wiped it over her body trying to pull away the sweat and fear that was clinging to her like wet mud. Without thinking, she became frenzied, wiping, brushing, rubbing the black teddy all over her body. Her movements were panicked and agitated without real purpose. She was losing control, wide-eyed, beginning to hyperventilate.

The hug around her arms pulling her close riveted Carol. Suddenly, any thought of moving forward with this mission had vanished, and she was looking everywhere around her, her eyes shifting with each jerk of the head.

Murphy pushed back gripping Carol's face.

"You're okay now, Carol. You're okay, look at me. You're okay."

Carol tried to twist her head from Murphy's grasp, afraid she'd miss the unseen ghost creeping up behind her.

Murphy persisted.

"Look at me, hey! I'm with you, you're okay. You are. Look down, Carol. You're naked, with me under-deck, and A-Okay." Murphy smiled and released her.

Carol focused on Murphy. She'd just met new-face but the trust in this woman's eyes began pulling the hysteria out of her chest. The enemy was close, but she had escaped. She did, and she was okay. She got out in time and wasn't a victim.

Murphy was new to this type of comforting. She'd learned a lot in the last eight months surrounded by Jennifer's team. It was not second nature for her to reach out to another person to offer support. The instinct it took was a learning process, but she smiled again when she saw Carol's eyes thank her.

All Murphy could say was, "You're welcome."

"I'm good, yeah," Carol took in a breath through her nose then exhaled. "I'm okay." She glanced down at the teddy gripping it in both hands. She rung out the sweat and felt the fear in her chest fall to the deck along with the drops of salty water.

SIX

"Carol," Jennifer Bane called out.

"Ahh!" Carol's eyes exploded open as she dropped the towel she was about to dry herself with. "Jennifer? You scared the shit out of me!"

Jennifer sat in the only chair in the small, dimly lit cabin aboard Rand Fullrider's attack light cruiser *Brandish*. Carol had exited the shower. She was dripping wet.

"Sorry," Jennifer stood, picked up the towel, and handed it to her. "Here."

Carol grabbed it but didn't use it, hesitating. She looked up into the taller woman's eyes. "Why in the world would you risk coming back on-station? Murphy and I snuck aboard Rand's ship coming up from under-deck."

Jennifer turned and sat back down. She exhaled.

"I have a very difficult time living in fear, Carol."

Carol absently brushed the towel down both arms studying Jennifer. She shuffled to the small bunk cubby on the bulkhead and sat down.

"I see. And your head, you aren't afraid of taking another pop to your top?" She dried her legs then the rest of her body and hair. She ran her fingers through her scalp smoothing it.

"Sure I am. Worried more than afraid, I'd say. It's just I can't—I mean I can't let you…" She trailed off, not certain how to say it.

"You don't want me to take all the risks."

Jennifer drew her lower lip between her teeth.

"Carol, I just met you. By accident at that, I heard about—I mean I know what you saw back there when you

60

reconned the Hair Raisers' hideout. This happens a lot around me. I'm like a friggin' magnet for this shit." Her face darkened. "I end up having to stop people that I don't choose to stop. My past is littered with people that get hurt working with me, or die working against me. It's so tiring I can't even begin to explain it."

"Jennifer, I'm not naïve." She reached for the shipboard grays beside her on the bunk putting them on. She bent over shoving both feet into a pair of low boots, then rested her hands on her legs. "Murphy told me I could bail anytime I wanted to. I'm sure that goes for this whole mess too. I see it in your eyes. You didn't force me to recon under-deck, did you?"

Jennifer didn't know what to say.

"So, can I go get some chow, or what?" She stood up. "You sitting there guilt-stricken is kinda turning my stomach." Her mouth curved up and hands shot to her hips. Carol was street smart and cagey. She was also older than Jennifer and had not led a sheltered life. She knew Jennifer was weakened but not *weak*.

Jennifer gave a lopsided grin. "Crafty shit storm, huh?"

"Correction—hungry shit storm." Carol jerked her head at the hatch.

Carol finished eating in the small galley then made her way to the cargo hold. Coming through the hatch she wiped at her mouth with a napkin then shoved it in a pocket.

"What's going on?" She surveyed the people standing just inside the hatch discussing something.

Basley Space Ops Commander Rand Fullrider had his back to the hatch when Carol entered. He turned to face her.

"Discussing next steps."

He pulled off his blue ball-cap and ran a hand through wavy brown gray-speckled hair.

"We don't have a full consensus on how to stop what you saw at the Hair Raisers, Carol." He popped the cap back on and crossed his arms. "I say it's never as simple as it looks.

Channing and Murphy tend to agree. But Jennifer here, well…" He shook his head, his gaze landing on Jennifer standing next to him.

Jennifer looked at Carol.

"Missions like these are always complicated, but that doesn't help the two people you saw, does it, Carol?"

Carol didn't know the man standing next to Murphy. He was about six-feet-two, older than Jennifer, and had the look of some type of law enforcement. Carol knew the type— analytical eyes, committed to preventing disaster, and all the backlash that came with that disaster.

Murphy saw the question on her face. "This is Channing Altimer, Carol."

Murphy wrapped an arm through Channing's elbow.

"My babe," she smiled. Murphy had put on blue trousers and a black hoody after cleaning up too.

"Hey, babe," Carol beamed at Channing. She turned to Jennifer. "What if the Hair Raisers use their speed, Jennifer?"

"What?"

"You said you were framed during the riot and that speed may have been a part of it. There's no other way that laser blade could have ended up in your hand, right?"

"No."

"Then if you force your way in to do a snatch-n-grab on those two very unfortunate people that are being tortured by the Hair Raisers, who's to say they won't take your head off, and hang you upside-down over a balcony?"

Carol had little tact. She wasn't indifferent though, not in the least. She was going to have a hard time forgetting the horrors she'd seen. That meant Jennifer needed to take a step back and not throw herself at this.

Jennifer blinked. Then her chest inflated. Suppressed outrage that time was being wasted leaked out in a huff.

Carol saw it.

"Look, don't go throwin' a wobbly, okay? You helped me yesterday. Now I'm just trying to help you. Dial it down some…please? Your effin' stare can burn skin."

Jennifer's jaw set, swishing around some saliva, then swallowed. She didn't admit defeat, but didn't admit she was wrong either.

Rand uncrossed his arms.

"I think Carol's suggestion goes for Biltmire Sta Sec too. If they go blundering in, after we tell them what's going on at the Hair Raisers' location, they're going to scare away the real catch—the top-dogs responsible for all this. What these people are doing could easily be taking shape off-station. We have no idea about the scale of their operation, none."

"Sta Sec are professionals, Rand." Channing reasoned. "They are."

This could be expected from Channing. He was a Detective Agent with Minos City Security on the planet Basley. He had faith in what pros could do; he was a part of that clique on his home planet, and believed in how his gang of do-gooders handled things.

"And we don't officially know that the Hair Raisers are the serial killers." All heads turned to Murphy. "Right?"

Silence.

"Scale, complexity…" Murphy gripped Channing's arm tighter for security.

"I'm worried about Sami," Jennifer said. "After I told her what Carol saw, we agreed it would be a good idea if she kept up her cover as a temp food worker. I'm not so sure that was a good idea now. Those Hair Raisers will be ordering more food and Sami will be delivering it tomorrow."

"Maybe we can use that to our advantage, Jennifer," Rand noted.

"How?"

Rand looked at Carol. "Maybe you could meet Sami when she docks and lace the food with ketamine."

Carol's eyes widened. "You mean try to knock those people out?"

Jennifer held up a hand.

"Wait a minute!" Her eyes bore into Carol. "You just warned me they might try to take my head off if I tried storming them." She turned to Rand. "Now, you want to throw Sami in there with no backup. No way, Rand, uh-uh!" Jennifer shook her head.

Carol reasoned, "Sami'll be expected to deliver food to whatever customers are on her run sheet. It would only make sense that the delivery supervisor would give her the same customers as today. Especially since she's new on the job."

Murphy chimed in, "I can hack into Food Theory's computer and change Sami's run sheet." She looked at Carol. "Or, you could do that, right, Carol?"

Carol nodded. "I could, but what good does that do?"

"By changing the run sheet, one of the other delivery workers will deliver food to the Hair Raisers. Sami won't go anywhere near them."

A bolt of panic hit Jennifer. "I don't want to leave that to chance, Murphy! What if the delivery supervisor changes her run sheet at the last minute? We don't have any control over that. I want her out of there. I was wrong to let her stay employed. With what Sami knows now, she might blow her cover when she comes face-to-face with these people again. It's human nature to be scared, and they may see it."

Carol cringed.

Jennifer noticed.

"What?"

The hairs on the back of Carol's neck stood up remembering what she saw.

"It's what they do."

"What?"

Carol's pupils flared.

"I saw what they do to people. They're experts at inflicting fear. Jennifer is right. They'll see it in Sami's eyes. Sami won't even know she's doing it, but these psychos will sense it. They'll smell the fear on her. I just know they will."

Jennifer snapped a look at Rand but he was already turning to leave through the hatch behind him.

Carol pulled her brows together into a frown.

"Where's he going? I can just contact Food Theory and have Sami fired. She won't even get on that cargo ship tomorrow."

Jennifer's mouth drew back showing her teeth.

"We leave *nothing* to chance when it comes to Sami, Carol. Rand is going to take *Brandish* to Food Theory Commodity Station and make sure Sami is safe. You have one job now. Your job is to contact Food Theory and stop her from getting on that cargo ship. You understand? That's your job, nothing else." Jennifer looked at Murphy and Channing, the two of them waiting.

Waiting for what Carol didn't know. Jennifer brushed past her and hit the down-ramp button next to the hatch. Jennifer turned and grabbed Carol's arm pulling her along following Murphy and Channing down the cargo ramp as it lowered.

At the bottom of the ramp Jennifer held up locking eyes with Carol.

"We're going to change ships. Marco is docked right next to us, one bay over. You and I can take the risk of being spotted by Sta Sec while we run the short distance to the docking bay next door. It's negligible."

Channing was already talking into a hand comp. He looked at Jennifer and nodded.

"Let's go!" He yelled.

The four of them sprinted down the port side of Rand's light cruiser. They could feel the fusion drive starting up with a rumbling hum that shook the landing bay deck under their feet. At the blast hatch, Murphy swung her hand over the scan pad and it opened. She stepped out onto the concourse street, scanned both directions, then motioned for all of them to follow. Channing jumped up behind Carol and Jennifer outstretching his arms to shield them close against his body.

"Snug tight and keep your heads down," he instructed the two women. They did. Murphy led the way taking a quick left out of the hatch. The next hatch up ahead was already open. The four of them rushed in, it closed.

Mia Julie, Marco's petite ebony first officer, was waiting just inside the docking bay. She signaled for the four of them to follow jogging in front to lead the way up the open cargo ramp into Marco's huge heavy battle cruiser. Up the ramp the pack went, the ramp already winding closed as the five of them jogged past the caution strips into the large cargo bay.

Carol followed along confused. *What's the urgency?* She thought. *With Rand going to Food Theory as a backup plan in case I don't get Sami fired first, why the panic?* She grabbed Jennifer's arm, pulling her to a stop.

"I'll contact Food Theory now. I can also logon and terminate her temp contract online."

"That's not all that's going to happen, Carol." Jennifer responded.

Murphy, Channing, and Mia stopped and turned, waiting.

Carol jabbed a look at them, then turned to Jennifer. Her jaw went slack finally understanding.

"You're going to try to rescue the two people that were being tortured by the Hair Raisers, aren't you?"

"Yes."

"But you can't! Didn't you listen to what I just said?"

"I'm not going to do this alone. Besides, I'm too big to climb up from under-deck."

"I thought you wanted me to make certain that Sami doesn't get on that cargo shuttle."

"Carol, I do, that is your job." Jennifer started to leave.

"Wait!" Carol still had hold of her arm. Murphy stepped over pulling Carol's grip from Jennifer's arm. Carol looked at Murphy.

Murphy reassured, "It's okay, Carol. I know the route to the wire raceway ladder under-deck you and I used to gain access to the Hair Raisers' location. And Krachy is a small man. He's going to go with me in your place."

"You people didn't even talk about this!" Carol almost shouted.

Jennifer swung her hand pushing at Carol's arm so she'd face her.

"Do you trust me?"

Carol's chest rose and fell. "Of course."

"Then come on, you need to get to work, and so do we." Jennifer tilted her head following Mia, Channing, and Murphy through the hatch. Carol fell in behind.

Krachy was waiting for them just through the hatch. This was the first time he'd seen Jennifer since she was arrested then escaped. He swung his arms around her then pushed back looking up into her eyes. "You being a good girl?"

Her mouth twisted. "Not really."

"Figures."

Jennifer and Krachy untangled and Krachy faced Carol. She was just three inches shorter than him. He extended a hand.

"Krachy Bantor."

Carol shook it.

"I feel like I know you even though this is the first time we met," Carol admitted referring to Krachy's position as Biltmire Station Director.

"Nice to meet you too."

Carol looked at Jennifer. "Where can I get started?" Almost before she finished the question, Channing was pulling her by the arm down the corridor.

Krachy looked at Jennifer. "What do you need me to do?"

Jennifer answered, "C'mon, the four of us have some planning to do."

Jennifer turned down the corridor in the opposite direction. She knew where she was going. Jennifer had spent years as a shipmate on *Baneful* when she was a part of Marco's crew in her early twenties.

Mia's first officer cabin was pretty spacious. Not that it mattered much to Mia. She was a small woman that had been first officer on Marco's ship for nearly seven years. What her cabin did have was a comp desk which all four of them were huddled around now.

Murphy sat at the comp desk tapping on the recessed keypad. Krachy was standing next to her leaning on an outstretched hand on the desk when he pointed at the screen.

"I think that's the circuit we'll need to deactivate," he commented.

Mia stood on the other side of Murphy and shook her head. "It won't cut the power to just the one retail shop."

Jennifer's hands rested on Murphy's shoulders standing behind her. She looked at Mia.

"Does that really matter?"

Mia shrugged. "Probably not, I'm just saying that if we cut the power on that circuit an entire section of retail shops are going to go dark."

Jennifer had proposed a plan to get the two torture victims back. The plan was to cause a diversion while Krachy attempted to extract the man and woman through the air vents in both rooms. The diversion was to cut the power to the retail store the Hair Raisers occupied.

Murphy stopped working the keypad.

"The key to this whole thing is to get the two victims alone in their rooms when Krachy grabs them. I have an idea about that."

She worked the keypad hard and in no time pulled up what she was looking for. She explained what was on the screen.

"These are the time tables for the Food Theory deliveries in that section of Biltmire today. What we can do is wait for the hot food to be delivered to the Hair Raisers. After the food is delivered, we wait a reasonable amount of time until the psychos sit down to eat their food together, then send Krachy in." She turned looking up at Krachy.

Krachy confirmed, "That'll help ensure that Bald Man and Stone-Face-Lady are not in the two torture rooms, but instead will be eating their meals in a common area."

Murphy turned back to the screen. "Food is delivered like clockwork by Food Theory. What's a reasonable period of time after the food is actually delivered before we should cut the power?"

Jennifer replied, "Krachy is only going to see one room at a time. When he sees Stone-Face-Lady leave the room to go eat her food, the hatch will lock. From what Carol said, there are two deadbolts on the hatch. Once the power is cut, Stone-Face-Lady can't get back into the room while Krachy is rescuing the victim because power controls the electronic hatch lock."

Mia scanned the others. "There are a lot of things that can go wrong with this plan." That also went for trying to decide on a reasonable period of time to wait before sending Krachy in. The list was long...

Jennifer pulled her hands off Murphy's shoulders and sat down on the bunk behind her. She rubbed her sore stomach.

"I know." She looked up at Krachy. "You sure you want to do this, love?" She just had to give him an out. If things had gone as planned today, the two of them would be married right now. The last two days *had* been a shit storm! This plan seemed like more of the same.

"How did you feel after you saved that little boy during the riot, Jennifer?" Krachy asked.

"Absolutely thrilled, euphoric even."

"I want that too." He smiled. "That'll make up for us not being married today, and then some."

Jennifer smiled. God she loved this man.

SEVEN

"You top-siders never ask us what's going on."

The voice behind them startled Murphy and Krachy as they turned a corner in the dark utilidor under-deck. Murphy's heart leaped in her chest as she spun around, but she didn't see anyone. Krachy, soldier-ready by habit, turned fast, his laser pistol out and aimed. The laser reticle was centered in the middle of the woman's forehead. Her face was peaking out from under a pipe above the corridor.

"Whoa there, Ser Bantor!" The woman's voice grew in volume. "You're tightened up like all buggery!" She looked down at Murphy. "Friend, *friend*, right, Murphy?"

Murphy shot a hand out signaling Krachy to stand-down. "I know her, Krachy."

Krachy eased off the trigger, the laser reticle disappearing. His shoulders sagged back to normalcy as he lowered the weapon.

"Hi, Lan," Murphy smiled as Lan extracted herself from her perch above the corridor and jumped down.

"Sorry 'bout that," Krachy said. "I'm a bit on edge."

"I gather," Lan gave him a guarded look. "You two aren't actually going to try use the same raceway top-side as Carol did to do her recon earlier are you?"

Krachy saw the foreboding in Lan's eyes. "Not now we aren't."

"Smart, 'cause after Carol and Murphy left, one of the creeps that Carol laid eyes on during her recon gifted us under-deckers with their oh so menacing presence."

Krachy's stomach clenched. "Shit!"

"Yeah, shit, Ser Bantor. You ready to listen now?"

"I'd love to, Lan. But there's a time factor here."

A line appeared between Lan's brows. "You're not calling in Sta Sec to help you?"

"If we do we might never get to the bottom of this. There's more to the serial killings than innocent dead people."

"I'm not surprised. All of us have heard the screams echoing down from top-side."

"We're going to try to rescue two people, Lan. Did the person that gifted you with their presence come down from top-side through the same raceway Carol used?"

"No, but we all know a new-face when we see one. This person showed up under-deck about an hour after Carol and Murphy finished their recon."

"What did she look like?"

"He, Ser Bantor, the guy was thin and bald."

"Shit!" Krachy pulled his lower lip under his teeth. "He must have known he was being spied on by Carol."

Lan scowled. "A lot of fuckin' good that did him. Freak Fams don't blow! We would never give up one of our own!"

"If Bald Man suspected, or even knew, that Carol had eyes on him from the air duct, he might have been on a fishing expedition coming down here to under-deck. Regardless, Murphy and I are still going to try to rescue the two people Carol saw being tortured. Can you help us gain access to the same air duct Carol used for her recon but from another direction?"

Lan's eyes rolled. "You don't want much, do you?" Anger clinched her jaw. "A lot of my friends were in the riot, you know. One of them didn't come back."

Murphy reached out performing greeting. Lan's tension ebbed a little. Murphy reassured her.

"We can do it ourselves, Lan." Her voice was strong with confidence, even though inwardly she had none—zero. It was a ploy. Murphy was using her freshly acquired interpersonal skills to tug at Lan's heart strings in an effort to get her to help.

Lan's eyes were icy, but there was sympathy behind them too. She was considering it.

Krachy knew what Murphy was doing. He did have to say that it was a very welcome surprise. Murphy had been all but incapable of compassion and teamwork when he first met her eight months ago. He pulled at her arm.

"Thanks, Lan. We gotta go." The two of them turned heading down the utilidor.

"Wait!" Lan blew out. "You fuckin' top-siders are gonna get yourself killed."

Krachy and Murphy turned taking several steps toward Lan. Krachy's eyes oozed compassion.

"I promise I'm ready to listen. To everything, and all of it, *after* you help us, Lan."

Lan's nostrils flared.

"What if you end up dead? Who's gonna listen then?"

Krachy tilted his head thinning his lips. He had no answer for that.

"Shit! This always happens when top-siders get involved. The tension mounts and my people suffer for it."

"I'm almost your people now," Krachy offered.

"What?"

"I won't be Station Director much longer."

"So, you think losing your job makes you an equal?"

"No, but it does drop me down a notch. Maybe the two lives we save shows I'm ready to risk it all to make things right."

"You haven't saved anyone yet."

"No, and I'd love to discuss this further, live down to your under-deck expectations, and generally not be the person you think I am, but my obligation to save two lives has been promised to the person that sprung Carol from detention. Which also happens to be the woman I wasn't able to marry today because she saved a little boy during the riot and got pinched for kidnapping doing it."

"Oh, cry me an effin' song, Bantor. You. Are. Breaking. My. Heart."

Krachy blinked. "What heart?"

Lan's mouth fell open. "Bastard!"

"No, Lan, I'm not a bastard, not even close. Bastards don't care."

"And you think I do?"

He closed in on her and performed greeting, like he'd done it all his life and maybe before that.

"Why have you let us do everything we do down here and never shut us down?"

"I already told you."

Lan's resistance was waning. Murphy was smart enough to keep her mouth shut and let it happen. Then Murphy saw Lan backing away from it. She wasn't convinced. Murphy tried one last thing to get Lan to help.

"Then take this and give it back to Carol if I don't come back."

She pulled the barbell nipple jewelry from her pocket and handed it to Lan.

Lan stared at the silver trinket in her palm. "I gave Carol this."

Murphy had no idea that was the case. All she said was, "Thank you, Lan."

"Bitch!" But Lan grinned when she said it.

Krachy let out the breath he was holding and shuffled one pace back against the utilidor wall.

Lan looked at him and dipped her head brushing past him. The two of them followed.

"If you make me regret this…" Lan didn't have a threat to issue because she was just one Freak Fam, and a loner at that.

***

Krachy looked up the ladder alongside the flexible metal conduit raceway Lan had stopped beneath, then back at her.

"You hate doing this, I get it, Lan. You can turn and leave the second I start climbing, but please, tell me again how to get to the Hair Raisers' location so I can burn the route into my memory."

A muscle in Lan's jaw twitched. "You're scared."

"You're scared for me. It's weighing me down and I don't have the strength, or room, to carry it with me up this ladder, please…"

Krachy was roping Lan in as much as he could. His legs were getting weak thinking about being stuck in a stupid box up there while spiders nibbled his bum. He came to the realization that his fear was heightened because unlike Carol earlier, he *did* know what might be waiting for him top-side.

Lan looked at Murphy. "You gonna to stay here while he plays super-saver?"

"First, I'm going to listen very carefully to everything you say, Lan. How you say it, and what you recommend when saying it, then yes, I'm going to wait for this Short Man Hunk to return because his woman will beat the snot out of me if I even think about leaving his narrow ass behind."

"A real woman would do it herself and not put him through this."

"It'd have to be a real small woman. Therefore, it falls to this real small man to do it instead."

"So what you're sayin' is you need me to make sure he doesn't screw the pooch." Lan scrunched up her face.

"You said it, I didn't. We may be at the point now that his life is in your hands."

Lan's lip lifted on one side. "And his narrow ass…"

"It's a nice ass, Lan. His woman has never caught me staring at it, which is why I'm as healthy as I am."

Krachy turned sideways and arched his behind. He kept his face neutral, which wasn't very hard given the circumstances.

"Fuckin' top-sider, he sure must be in love. This is beyond sacrifice." Lan's eyes dropped scrutinizing what Murphy had in her hand. "So what are those, then?"

"Sub-vocal mic and earbud. Can I show you how they work?"

Lan nodded reluctantly.

Murphy pressed the small mic to Lan's throat then pushed one of the earbuds into an ear.

Lan touched at the mic on her throat then shook her head side-to-side to convince herself it would stay in place. She spoke at regular voice. Krachy gestured for Lan to talk lower. She did. He already had the earbud in and nodded.

"Yeah, that's better, Lan. They're very sensitive. You only need to whisper."

Some color drained from Lan's face.

"You're really going to do this with my help, aren't you?"

Krachy forced a weak smile. He had to push it onto his lips.

"Teamwork is a wonderful thing, Lan."

"Don't get misty on me," she scoffed. "Tell me when you reach the second cable-way. Turn right into that second duct. You won't have to worry about sound because that crawlspace is ceramacrete not metal. When you come to the next intersection, the left turn you make will squeeze you into the metal air duct maze that leads to their hide-out. I'll guide you from there."

Murphy looked at her hand comp.

"Krachy, food will be delivered to the Hair Raisers in about 30 minutes."

She looked at Lan. "That's enough time for him to get in place, right?"

Lan nodded. "Plenty, should only take 10 or 15 to get in position."

Krachy reached up for the ladder pulling himself higher. He transformed his mind into battle-mode, had to. What he'd said earlier to Lan was true. There was no room for anyone else's fear on this trip but his own. After several deep breaths, his senses were peaked. He was too much of a pig-headed man to admit he was downright terrified of spiders. Now he was crawling right toward a place where they were being used as ammunition. *WTF?*

Krachy concentrated, one hand on the ladder, one foot next. The thought of Sami being the person delivering the food to the Hair Raisers was not permitted. He trusted Jennifer's team and began to relax knowing at least *that* part of the equation was calculated in his favor. Sami was far away from here. Krachy was certain of it.

After more than 15 minutes of instruction from Lan, he was just one bend in the air duct from the first torture room vent—Bald Man room. Krachy had on a form-fitting black micro fiber long sleeve shirt and stretch leggings. The clothes gave him a few advantages. The wicking nature of the fabric pulled sweat away from his body. He wasn't sticking to the metal surface of the air duct. The clothes were also comfortable and gave him a full range of motion to allow him to slide silently, as long as he crept along at a snail's pace. Lastly, the tight neck line of the shirt allowed him to stash his L pistol on his back, up between his shoulder blades, for easy access.

The plan was to wait "a reasonable period of time" after the food was delivered by a Food Theory worker before cutting the power. This would hopefully ensure that all the Hair Raisers had gathered to eat their meal together leaving the torture victims alone in their rooms. Then start the rescue.

Krachy got a confirm from Lan, that "a reasonable period of time" was one minute away. In a minute the power would be cut. He was now committed, took in a shallow breath, then eased himself forward around the bend leading to Bald Man room. Krachy hesitated as he pulled himself around the bend. That's when he saw it—A thin beam of light was visible against his leading wrist not eight inches from his face.

Fresh fear reared up within Krachy at the realization—motion activated sensor! His rising panic fueled a desperate grab behind his head snatching the laser pistol. No sooner than he had the weapon in his grip he saw movement. The grate up ahead spilled light on them scratching against the metal floor of the duct coming his way. Then a few of them crawled up each side of the duct as if surrounding their prey in a coordinated attack. The light coming in from the grate glinted off all eight legs of each dark, hairy brown spider. Bald Man had set a motion activated spider trap!

Krachy knew his terror was real. His bum really was going to get nibbled by spiders, if they even made it down his body that far before sinking their fangs into his flesh. He was face-to-face with the first one creeping its way directly toward his nose. It was as though the cluster of eight eyes arranged in rows on the creature's head was staring him down. He looked straight into the grotesque eyes of the closest spider against his free will. Far too close—he could almost see his reflection in the largest two round bulging orbs on its head. All he could think was: *I'm in a metal box with nowhere to go.*

Krachy forced his clinched jaw slack so he wouldn't bite through his tongue...*This is really going to hurt!*

Krachy pressed the tip of the LP barrel against the metal duct floor, snapped his eyes shut, then squeezed the trigger.

The electrical shock through the thin metal all around him sounded like a firecracker. The duct around him lit up with charged energy sending a wicked bolt of surging current in every direction singeing the spiders and popping them off the metal like popcorn exploding to release kernels. Unfortunately, it did the same to Krachy. He had almost nowhere to bounce except strait up. The lightning field surged through his chest, hips, and legs slamming him up into the roof of his metal box with a whip-snapping crack.

"Ahhhhh!" He screamed then passed out from the muscle clinching jolt. He came to rest.

Krachy opened his eyes and the burnt smell hit him. He swallowed back a retch. He focused ahead. An inch from his nose was a shriveled, smoldering, arachnid. All eight legs were curled tight into its chest like a flower petal that closed due to lack of sun. Krachy flicked it away with a finger. Its crispy shell skittered across the air duct, ping-ponging off two more dead bugs, spinning like a top, then stopped.

He relaxed his body and hugged the floor of his box like a lost friend. In and out his breath started to pull some strength back into his limbs. His cheek rested on the floor. Just in front of his face was a now useless sub-vocal mic. The plasti shell of the small white button was melted. He reached up digging in his ear to pull out the useless earbud. On his own, with no more instructions to help him, he realized that a second assault wave might be headed his way, so he focused ahead at the grate.

"Who's up there!? Please, I can hear you! Help, help me!" A shaky, strained voice drifted in from the grate.

Then the world went black. The power was cut. With no more dim light spilling in, Krachy reached in the lone zippered pocket on the back of his legging and pulled out a small LED headlamp. Fingers crossed in his mind, he turned it on. Although small, the handy light snapped on sure and strong flooding his box with brightness. It was a low tech device which proved its worth. It didn't short circuit during the laser-bolt-energy-jolt. He put it on.

Quickness was required now. Krachy pulled himself level with the grate and shouldered the thin metal screen five times, grunting loud as the edges gave way and it sprung out of its frame.

Krachy's light beam landed on the man strapped to the operating table below. Panic from the man's eyes jabbed looks at the rolling cart next to the op table, then back at Krachy. For a moment Krachy thought the man was looking at the hatch afraid someone was coming through it. But he wasn't. His head darted again and again toward the cart, then back at

Krachy. All the while he licked his lips in what seemed like anticipation.

Krachy extracted himself from the vent ass first and landed on his feet.

"Stop, stop!" He grabbed the side of the man's face trying to calm him. The LED beam pierced the man's pupils, constricting them to pinpricks. "Can you climb?"

The man's head jerked up-and-down in Krachy's grasp.

Krachy had the arm and leg buckles off fast. As soon as the restraints were off, the agitated man lunged for the cart with the syringes and vials on top grabbing a handful, then stood up. As he did, one of the vials fell out of his grasp and landed on the operating table.

Krachy saw the man standing by the table licking his lips and figured he was ready to escape. By impulse, Krachy turned and picked up the vial the man dropped to bring it along too.

When Krachy spun around, the man was not standing behind him any longer. The corners of the room were dark so he aimed the headlamp in every direction. He even looked straight up—nothing. Krachy frowned as his light framed the vent up above and figured the man must have already crawled up and through. He didn't understand how that could have happened. He didn't hear anything, and he'd only turned his head for a split second to grab the vial.

Fighting confusion wrapped with urgency, Krachy shoved the single ampule of medicine in his back pocket. He zipped it shut then jumped up and pulled himself into the vent only to find the man gone. He didn't hear a sound in the metal air duct in either direction. No echo of a crawling person, just an eerie silence.

Still perplexed, Krachy's beam turned left. He pushed a few dead spider carcasses out of his way and crawled fast to Stone-Face-Lady's room up ahead. No sound escaped from the vent as he ventured a glimpse through the grate. His beam landed on a woman, either dead or unconscious, hanging as he had been told by Carol, in the square fixture. He shouldered the grate out of its frame, jumped down into the room, and reached up placing two fingers on the woman's throat.

His heart surged in his chest. The woman was still alive. Her wrists and ankles were a mess of bleeding cuts and scabs. She had been tortured many times. Anger added to urgency as Krachy freed the woman from her bonds, slung her over his shoulder, then pulled the control desk from the other side of the room under the vent. He tossed the woman on the desk, jumped up himself, then heaved her with a grunt up into the opening. He pushed her ass, then the back of her thighs and legs forcing the limp awkward body into the air duct channel to the left.

Krachy was dripping with sweat when he pulled himself into the vent in front of the woman. She was at his feet. The only way he could gain enough leverage to pull him and her through the duct was to loop both feet down into the woman's armpits as he clawed his way forward with all his strength. He dragged her along behind him in the tight confines of the metal box.

With no help forthcoming from Lan, Krachy struggled onward. On his journey in, he had etched an arrow with the sharp front site of his LP. He had used the tip of the site like a knife to scratch a directional arrow at each bend in the tunnel so he could find his was out.

Panting, grunting, he finally came to the vertical ladder raceway leading down to under-deck. His headlamp shot down the raceway and landed on Murphy's face as she pulled herself up the ladder to help him. Krachy started to feel relief that he was going to get the woman out. He heard a stir in the duct behind him, then a flitter of what sounded like the tiny feet of a child against the ceramacrete crawl-space. The faint sound receded in an instant, then was gone. Silence.

Krachy lifted an elbow to look behind him in the cable-way. The woman was gone.

EIGHT

Krachy had little to show for his adventure, or so he thought. He did have sore muscles, a hammering heart, pride he got the two people out, and a pharmaceutical ampule of clear liquid which he trusted with Murphy so she could rush it back to Marco's ship for analysis. Murphy headed off down the dim utilidor and was out of sight fast. Krachy fell back against the wall placing outstretched hands on his knees. He tried to catch his breath, sweat mixed with bewilderment and relief that he'd made it out alive. The emotion puddle between his feet grew as it rained down from his nose.

Lan looked down at him.

"You still haven't saved anyone yet."

Krachy didn't have the strength to right himself and smack the smirk off her face. He took a queue from Murphy's newly found talent of using interpersonal skills instead.

"Thank you for your help," he managed between breaths.

Lan didn't expect that.

"But I lost contact with you. Murphy couldn't take it any longer and started to climb up to see what happened."

Head still down, "I got them both out," Krachy hocked a loogie.

"Where are they?"

Krachy stood up.

Lan swallowed. What Krachy was carrying inside him was radiating off his body like a malignant spirit. She felt the snug thread of distrust toward top-siders unwrap around her until she was no longer the defiant woman that Krachy met earlier. She was someone that understood now. Someone connected. Someone who was *almost* capable of trust.

A teammate?

Lan's whole face lit up. Krachy saw it.

"That feeling is new, but you'll let it settle in before long." He brushed his arm across his face a few times.

Lan's lips pursed, like she was disappointed even though they both knew the two lives she'd help save meant Krachy did risk it all to make things right.

"Three, Lan," Krachy coughed, his breath slowing.

"Three?"

"You helped save my life too." He flopped his hands open palms up. "I'm still here. And that was no guarantee."

"I think I underestimated you."

"Not really. I think you were fighting it."

"Fighting what?"

"Being my friend."

"So, you think we're friends now?"

"I have no intention of telling what I saw to a stranger."

"Trustwords?"

Krachy lifted his shirt and rubbed his face. When his shirt came down, Lan paled under his earnest look.

"I can't tell you about my past. If I open that up on top of what I just saw, I won't be able to think straight."

"I definitely underestimated you."

Krachy's renewed panic about being locked in a box with spiders was making him sweat again.

Lan rose a finger toward his face. "Your eyebrows are crusty..."

He didn't know what she meant at first, then his eyes rolled toward his brow.

"I'm terrified of spiders. There, I said it. I electrocuted every one of the little bastards and have no remorse about it at all. You're the only person that knows that deep dark secret.

Unfortunately, I zapped my own ass too." He brushed at his brows. Black, crispy flakes puffed out into a mist disappearing in the dim light. "I need to sit down before I fall down."

Krachy fell down.

"Too late." He hated using the ploy, but Lan was wasting too much time. He needed her to spill what she knew, and he needed her to do it soon. He looked his thanks up at her and grunted as she helped him stand. The grunt was real. The laser jolt that riddled his muscles still hurt.

Lan had her arm around his waist. His arm was draped over her shoulder as they stood. He was wet and warm against her body. She had almost no clothes on. He looked into her eyes.

"I'm not dead and I'm ready to listen, Lan."

She didn't extract herself from his grip. Her face contorted, then the breath she let out pulled the white flag of truce she'd been protecting up the flag pole.

"Follow me."

***

The square hatch at the top of the ladder raceway Krachy and Lan arrived at opened into a small, back storage room. From the smell the place was a coffee shop. Krachy bent down and offered a hand to Lan, which she took, to help her standing.

Lan could tell he was running on fumes. Krachy shuffled over to the lone chair next to the wall, shrugged forward, his elbows on his knees, head down. He was exhausted.

Krachy jerked his eyes open at Lan's touch as she dabbed his brow with a server's towel. She wrapped a blanket around him. The smell of fresh coffee lifted his head.

Lan saw the question on his face. "It's decaf."

He smiled weakly and grabbed the mug and a croissant sandwich she handed to him. He attacked both.

Lan nodded, satisfied so far. She was around 40 years old with pale cream skin and dark black eyebrows under two black French braid pigtails that ran down over each breast. Her dark eyes were street-wise and the thin crimson lips she sported gave her face a young edge. She slipped off each black flat with a toe pull at the ankle, then took off the chain detail halter bodysuit from around her neck. The black mesh halter only hid what was under the four looping, thin silver chains over her breasts, which was not much. Down it went over her hips and dropped to the floor.

Krachy concentrated on his meal as she grabbed a pair of trousers and T-shirt off a clothes hook.

She pulled on the pants and shirt then flipped her two pigtails out of the collar.

"I work here." She slipped on the flats.

He finished taking a drink. "Where we at? Holy Grounds or Mellow Brew?"

Her mouth twitched, "Holy Grounds."

Krachy stood up finished with his sandwich. He had to look up at her. She was five-seven. He sniffed.

"The smell is exquisite."

"C'mon," she led the way out the hatch into the barista station. "Go take a seat in a booth."

The smell *was* exquisite. Krachy needed to calm his nerves and confusion. How was he going to explain what he'd just seen the two people do during the rescue? One second the two people were next to him, then the next they vanished. He bent into a booth on the wall and sat down as far back from the entrance as possible. He wanted to see the entrance and everyone and everything. His anxiety to have a clear view after being locked in a carton with spiders was making him start to sweat again. He wiped at his forehead with the blanket.

Lan studied Krachy as she came around the barista counter before stepping over to the booth.

"Easy," she said seeing his tension. She sat another cup o' joe and a croissan'wich in front of him. She took the seat across from him and folded her small hands.

He chomped away, then washed it down with gulps.

"It wasn't just the spiders that's got me frantic, Lan," he managed around a mouthful.

"We're both safe."

Krachy knew that was true. No one was staring but it was clear Lan was among her people, other Freak Fams. He was starting to feel better.

She sat patiently, as though waiting for him to finish his food. But there was more to it than that, a lot more. Her eyes bore into him.

"I'm just learning my way around the real Biltmire Space Station. The Freak Fam is only one of many groups."

Krachy swallowed another mouthful looking at her.

"I can see you want me to get on with it, and hey, for you that's fine. Yeah, just fine for you. But where does that leave me? You get to lock yourself behind top-side hatches. I can't."

The doubt she had adhered to her like a medal won in battle. Lan had earned her life and didn't want to retreat from it to help him. Krachy was safe. She would not be. He couldn't disagree with that. He wasn't going to deny it either. But he did think he knew what *part* of her reluctance was.

"I think you mean you won't, right?"

"Won't what?"

"I get that you want to continue to live your life the way you do, Lan. You've fought hard for the privilege. I'm not belittling that."

Her jaw clinched and she rose off the bench a few inches.

"Yes. You. Are!" She snapped.

"How many times am I going to have to explain myself to you?"

Lan eased back down. "You sit there like I should believe anything and everything you say. I just met you."

"Oh please, no you didn't."

She knew what he meant. "So I've seen you run things around here as space station director. I even know you tossed the former director out an airlock then took his place during a hostile takeover."

"You and I both know that guy was a fuckin' asshole."

Lan gritted her teeth. "That's what I mean about you…"

She was having a tough time forming it on her lips. She just couldn't say his first name. The fact that Krachy could discharge people with such ease was not enhancing her calm. If he was going to get to the bottom of what Lan knew it had to start with trust. Just had to.

"Krachalavito Bantor, pleased to meet you, Ms. Chevron." He pulled his hand from under the blanket.

She looked at it, only a hint of surprise on her face that Krachy knew her last name.

He flicked a look at his hand then back at her.

"Go ahead, it's wet 'n clammy, but given freely. No strings." He smiled crookedly.

The long breath she exhaled felt warm on his hand. She shook it. He didn't linger in FF connect. They released. He wanted to show respect. She deserved that.

Krachy could not waist anymore time. One, because his energy reserves were depleting, and two, it was now or never.

"You won't give up what you know because you think that by doing so, I will betray that trust. That I will, in some way, toss you out an airlock like I did to that little shit Bontrava a few years ago when I took over as director. Those are valid fears, Lan. I am not minimizing what you've accomplished to make yourself happy. That's not such an easy thing to do living your whole life in space. I came from Basley, so ultimately I'm a dirt-sider. I took over the job here because I didn't trust anyone else to do it right. The men under me when I was commanding Station Security were scared to rebel against my coup just like you're scared to trust me now. Have you ever seen or heard of anyone trying to assassinate me for what I did?"

"No."

"That should tell you that, on the whole, I've done a good job as station director. It should also tell you that Sta Sec would rather work under my guidelines than someone else's. Finally, it should tell you that I successfully coerced Station Security to stay out of the business of groups like the Freak Fam. Because it's none of their damn business how you live your lives as long as you don't hurt anyone doing it. I personally made the Freak Fam take their raves under-deck two years ago so the tight-ass top-siders on-station would keep paying taxes to support everyone around them including you. It's a real simple system and it works. The system even works for the group you're scared to tell me about—the VG."

Her lips drew back. "You already know about them!?"

Krachy was trying be patient. He didn't let out the sigh he wanted to. The man Lan was talking to was the director of the entire space station. Of course he knew about the VG.

"Yes, I know. But what I don't know is what you know."

Her eyes widened.

"That's right, Lan. I don't know who to ask permission from to stop all the fuckers that are practicing their serial killing techniques on OUR station. You know who that person is, who the leader of the VG is, I don't!"

"So you're going to just walk in there by yourself and ask this leader for permission to cut off a part of their income stream?"

"Unless you're coming with me, yes."

"The serial killings may be many things, Krachy," she almost spit out the name, "but they are also a source of revenue for the VG. Not their biggest source, but a source, nonetheless. It always comes back to creds, *always*."

"It sure does."

"If I tell you the name of the leader of the VG, what's to keep it from coming back at me. I'm only 41 freakin' years old!"

"Do you think the VG have eyes on you right now?"

"Why would they? I'm nobody. But the Freak Fam aren't. I spill and it comes back at them. I won't do that. They're family."

"What if in asking permission I replace the VG's lost revenue so it won't come back at the Freak Fam?"

"They won't buy that bill of goods, Krachy. No way!"

"You just said it all comes back to creds. The VG are business people."

"You're forgetting about their honor bound blood oaths. If the group doing the killings on-station have been given permission by the VG, then that group has taken a blood oath too. They'd have to have taken the oath to be allowed to operate on a space station controlled by the VG."

"You're forgetting something—Station Security has a say in this too. They're going to take out the VG, surgically remove the organization from the bottom-up."

"What?"

"It's going to happen soon. I won't be a part of it. Sta Sec has an independent charter. Law enforcement is law enforcement. I have limited control over Station Security as director. The riot tipped the pendulum too far. Sta Sec figure if they take out the VG, all of it goes away, the serial killings, all of it."

"Why is that a bad thing then?"

"Because, Lan, some other group will swoop in and fill the void taking the VG's place. Who knows what kind of people they'll be? Who knows what kind of *beings* "it" will be? The VG, while their methods are often questionable, do own legitimate businesses, perform charitable acts, and are mostly involved in white-collar type crime. They operate restaurants, bars, cargo transports, and may even have a stake in Food

Theory. I know the drugs floating around come in from them. And there's other criminal activity they run too. What they don't do is partner with slavers. That's against the VG's code of honor. Slavers deal in human trafficking and downright human misery." Krachy looked around the café and exhaled. "I'd like to help keep it that way."

"Why did you risk your life to save those two people? Saving them wouldn't help shut down the group doing the serial killings."

Krachy shook his head. "I've tried to explain that to you. Carol thought it was important enough to risk her life. You still don't want to believe either of us. Why?"

Lan's eyes burned with recognition. "You really do care."

"Carol risked her life to help my fiancée. When Carol discovered that two people were being tortured, I couldn't let her sacrifice be for nothing. So I risked my life to save them. Trying to save them was the right thing to do. Saving those people was never going to shut down the group doing the killings, but it could have made a difference to the two people. I hope it does…"

"Where did they go, Krachy?"

"I told you that I would not tell that to a stranger. Are you a stranger, Lan?"

This was it. He held his breath. He didn't care if she saw it or not.

Lan shook her head. "No."

Krachy told Lan everything about the two people that disappeared during the rescue attempt.

Lan told Krachy who the leader of the VG was.

NINE

Despite Lan's assurance of safety, leaving Holy Grounds by the front entrance seemed foolish. If the VG suspected that a leak about their organization came from the Freak Fam, walking out the front entrance would draw unwanted attention. This was the FF's gathering spot. Krachy was a figurehead on Biltmire. The math was easy.

Survival was the plan and the immediate goal. Krachy was a foot soldier by trade. Progress from A to B, with he and Lan in tact. Until the VG allowed an equitable end to the serial killings, they would protect the income stream it provided. Whatever that income stream was, and how it connected to torturing and killing innocent people over the last month, didn't matter at the moment.

Lan returned to their booth after speaking with several people in the café.

Krachy pulled the blanket off. He was nearly dry now and the food he ate had given him much needed energy. He looked past Lan as almost the entire café emptied single file out the hatch behind the barista station. Something like awe transformed his face as he looked up at her.

Lan shrugged. "You have your team, I have mine."

"How long do they need to set-up?"

"Not long. I told them where we're headed. They'll pick the route, not me. They spot any new-faces and we'll be rerouted under-deck."

And they were. The journey through under-deck back to Marco's heavy battle cruiser, *Baneful*, was without incident.

Krachy knew that Lan had carefully considered telling him about the leader of the VG before doing so, and he admired her for that.

He grabbed her elbow. She turned. Their eyes locked in a shared understanding.

"I thought it through, Krachy. Sometimes you just have to go for it."

***

It seemed like all the women in Krachy's life were strong. When he and Lan stepped up the last rung of the ladder from under-deck into Marco's docking bay, the look Krachy saw on Jennifer's face made him rethink that.

"Sami's missing," Jennifer said without preamble. She turned and led the way up the cargo ramp into Marco's ship.

Marco stood next to Mia Julie waiting for Jennifer, Lan, and Krachy. Marco explained.

"Rand landed on Food Theory. He verified that Sami's temp contract was terminated by Carol. Problem was, Sami was not on the cargo ship when it docked on Food Theory. After Sami completed delivering food, she got on the cargo transport to return to Food Theory but was not on the ship when it docked."

Krachy looked at Lan.

Lan returned his nervy look. "You told me the VG had legitimate businesses…"

She didn't finish her sentence letting Krachy fill in the rest.

"Oh no, I guessed the VG might have a stake in Food Theory. I just didn't think I was right." Krachy's heart jumped.

Jennifer tried to reassure her man.

"Krachy, how could you have known?" She would be damned if she was going to let Krachy blame himself after

92

what he'd already been through. Murphy told Jennifer what happened to him during the rescue attempt.

Marco regarded Lan. "Lan, I'm Marco. This lady beside me is Mia."

Lan scanned them both with a nod then clapped her eyes on Jennifer.

"Thank you for looking after Krachy. I'm Jennifer."

Lan cast an analytical eye. "You the fiancée, then?"

Jennifer nodded. "Carol's on-board." She turned to Marco. "I'll get her and meet all of you in the ward room." Jennifer turned fast heading for the hatch.

Before the others started to follow, Krachy pushed his way past Marco and Mia catching up with Jennifer. Just through the hatch, she spun around and clamped onto Krachy with a crushing embrace.

Krachy wrapped his arms around her. *What a terrific hug,* he thought. The hug morphed into a *I can't believe you're still alive hug*—awesome.

They pulled back. "Thrilling but not euphoric," Krachy rated the rescue.

Sadness clouded Jennifer's features. "I'm sorry, love."

"Nothing to be sorry about. I got them both out at least."

"I never doubted you would." Her hands drifted to his cheeks before she gently released them turning to go get Carol. Jennifer didn't say anything about Krachy's singed eyebrows.

The only light on in Carol's cabin was a night-light over the mirror in the head. Jennifer could hear the water running in the shower, but then it stopped. She was momentarily distracted by a nagging thought—*Why was Carol taking a shower?*

Too long. When Jennifer didn't hear the retractable shower door open, the first faint clamor of alarm bells went off in her mind.

She threw herself across the intervening space and reached for the shower door handle. Jennifer caught movement in the mirror. It was Carol closing in fast from behind with a laser blade held high in her hand.

Jennifer spun watching the deadly shank rocket down past her face slicing the garrote the man was about to wrap around her neck. The man had lunged out of the shower past the now open shower door. The taught wire snapped, then the man shoved both women sideways, plunging them into empty space between the toilet and wall.

The toilet seat clipped Jennifer sharply on the side of the head and knocked her unconscious.

Carol sputtered underneath. All the air pushed out of her lungs.

***

Jennifer fluttered her eyes open then squeezed them shut. Even the dim light in Marco's Medico sent shockwaves of pain through her skull.

A rush of coolness flooded her forearm then surged up her shoulder from the IV that was inserted in Jennifer's vein. After two more gulps of air, the calming wave enveloped her chest and head. Her muscles released and she let out a slow breath. Her nausea ebbed as she nodded off.

***

Carol and Lan sat next to each other at a table in the ward room on *Baneful* watching Marco pace back-and-forth. Mia sat across from them.

Anger pulsed off Marco pushing a wave of heat Carol and Lan could almost feel as he turned and stalked back down the aisle again. He was furious with himself for allowing an assassin to sneak aboard his ship. Worst of all, the killer almost succeeded! If not for Carol, the killer would have ended Jennifer's life.

Murphy entered through the hatch.

"This is the third time they've tried to scare Jennifer off, maybe the fourth. Kidnapping Sami may be a warning too. Who knows? Whoever is behind this has to know we're close to figuring out what this is all about, even though none of this shit makes much sense. How are they making a profit killing innocent people? Even I don't understand that."

Krachy came in the open hatch and scanned the others; he brushed past Murphy then sat down next to Mia.

"Jennifer is resting. The doctor's making sure she's not in pain." He bit at his lip. "He doesn't know how bad her head is, but he said she wouldn't be this sick unless this was cumulative head trauma."

Carol shifted in her chair.

Krachy was so tense he spotted it. His eyes locked onto her face, but she wouldn't look at him.

"What, Carol? You know something."

Lan glanced at Carol. "Carol?"

Krachy pressed further, "You just saved Jennifer's life. Tell me."

Carol looked at Krachy.

"I promised I wouldn't say anything."

Her head was spinning too. She'd seen Jennifer go into the cabin then followed her in. Marco had given her the laser blade as a precaution and told her to keep it ready. How right Marco was to be paranoid was all too clear now. As soon as Carol came through the hatch in the cabin, she saw movement next to Jennifer. The thought of a person trying to pull a wire across Jennifer's throat flipped a switch in Carol's brain she didn't know existed. The next few seconds were nothing but rage—pure rage. The instant she saw movement to Jennifer's left, her blood turned to ice. The rest was reflex.

"I promised Jennifer. I knew it was a stupid promise when I made it. She's really sick, Krachy. I was so upset when I saw her come back on-station—I just knew something like this was going to happen," she shook her head, "I just knew it!"

"Tell me."

Carol swallowed not finding the words. Lan nudged her with an elbow. Carol regarded her and Lan lifted her head in Krachy's direction. Carol didn't want to be the deliverer of such bad news.

"I noticed it during our escape yesterday…Look, I don't want to tell you. Can't you just ask Jennifer when she wakes up?" Even as she asked, she knew that was a pipe dream. Jennifer would never admit her weakness.

Krachy's look said the same thing—pipe dream.

"After Jennifer took the shot to her stomach, she almost passed out trying to get us out of detention. She didn't think I noticed her slurred speech, but I did. I asked her how bad it was when we were safe on her ship *Viper II,* but all she did was make me promise to keep it a secret. What was I supposed to do?" Carol's eyes were pleading.

"I'm not blaming you, Carol. I know how Jennifer is," Krachy reassured.

Carol leaned forward on her elbows.

"You need to get her far away from here, Krachy."

"You try." His brow lifted.

"Then just keep her drugged and make her leave!"

Lan spoke up.

"How about just finishing this damn thing so Jennifer doesn't get hurt again! You guys ever think of that?" She spat.

Mia added, "Before we go there, you need to know what Murphy brought back from the Hair Raisers. I had the doctor analyze the vial of drugs. The doctor said the medication is a form of immunosuppressant. The drug in that vial helps stop a person's body from rejecting a new organ and any infection that comes along with it."

Marco studied her.

"Are you talking about rejection drugs?"

"Yes," Mia replied.

Carol chimed in, "I saw Bald Man tell the man he was torturing that the rejection drugs were not going to be withheld. He even injected the man with a dose. It sounded like Bald Man was using the threat of withholding the rejection drugs along with using the spiders to make sure the man conformed. Bald Man said there would always be ways to make people conform. Conform to what I don't know."

"What about the woman that was being tortured?" Krachy asked.

Carol thought back remembering.

"The woman was terrified of heights. Stone-Face-Lady was moving her up and down in that cage to scare her. Stone-Face-Lady wanted the woman to conform too. I also remember the woman saying that she was in pain."

"What pain?" Mia asked.

"Internal pain, like she was rejecting whatever Stone-Face-Lady put inside her. She was begging to be given a dose of the rejection drugs. The woman said she'd conform but needed the drugs because of the pain. It was awful, Mia."

Lan was watching Carol as she explained. She knew her well.

"What else, Carol? You remember something else don't you?"

Carol turned to Lan.

"I do. Stone-Face-Lady told that poor woman that it was all up to her how the torture ended."

"Well, she's not being tortured now," Krachy concluded.

Carol turned to him. "What if the woman that was being tortured goes back?"

"What?"

"I said what if the woman and man you rescued are in so much pain from the organs, or whatever, that's been implanted inside them, that they have to go back. They have to go back to the people that tortured them to receive the rejection drugs to make the pain go away."

Krachy's brow furrowed.

"But that would mean they'd be tortured again with acrophobia and arachnophobia."

"Maybe the pain is so bad it's worth the risk, Krachy," Carol reasoned.

"Maybe it is," a strong voice behind Marco said. All of them turned seeing Jennifer standing just inside the hatch. She was holding what looked like an iced down cocktail in one hand. She took a long pull, then walked over to the table and sat down next to Krachy. She looked at Carol. When she did she burped. "Sorry," she said as if nothing had happened. "Carol, what can I say? I didn't see that guy trying to kill me. You did. Thank you!"

Carol was a bit confused as she watched Jennifer finish off the amber liquid, plopping the empty glass on the table.

"Are you okay, Jennifer?"

"As you all know now—no, I am not okay," she dug in her pocket and pulled out the prescription meds Russell Sauchen had given her back on *Viper II*. She set the bottle on the table.

"I'm pretty doped up and the bourbon feels great mixed with the drugs." She turned to Krachy. "Not euphoric, but close."

Krachy looked over at Carol. "See what I mean."

"I saw it on Ian's face yesterday, Krachy. She IS always like this, huh?"

Krachy squeezed Jennifer's hand. "My woman." He eyed her warily.

"Lan," Jennifer looked at her, "I don't want you to think I rope people into my problems just because they helped save my Short Man Hunk's narrow ass."

Jennifer flicked a look at Murphy. Murphy pulled her lips together. Jennifer turned back to Lan.

"So anytime you want out, you say the word." She scanned the others. "I just want all of you to know that I am now officially pissed off! This shit with people trying to kill me *and* having the nerve to kidnap one of my friends stops now." Jennifer's body wasn't coiled like a spring due to the drugs and alcohol, but her eyes could have melted dura steel into flowing droplets of bright-hot molten metal. "Time to go on offense!"

Lan thought for a moment and replied.

"Your Short Man Hunk didn't exactly rope me in. I thought long and hard about what I was going to tell him before I joined the effort. I will say that you people seem to me like you're just spinning your wheels on this. It's no wonder you almost got killed again today, Jennifer."

It was then that Krachy realized that Lan had NOT told him everything she knew about the VG when the two of them talked at Holy Grounds earlier.

Lan looked at him. "Don't stare an effin' hole through my head, Bantor!"

Jennifer was quick on the uptake, which, given her condition, was quite the accomplishment. She slung her arm around Krachy's shoulder feeling his warmth. She looked at Lan.

"I thought Carol was the only crafty shit storm under-deck?"

"You would be wrong," Lan smirked.

"Let me ask you this, Lan," Lan pushed herself back in her chair as though she knew what was coming. What was coming was another question that she'd rather not answer, be expected to answer, and probably wouldn't answer. Just like the conversation with Krachy at Holy Grounds. Her looked became defensive. "How does someone make money killing innocent people?"

That was not the question Lan anticipated. "Well, I—I'm not sure how."

"You're right, they don't, Lan. That's why you don't know how."

"You're saying I'm right? What?" Lan was confused. So was everybody else.

Jennifer looked up at Marco. Marco didn't know the answer, but what Jennifer saw in his eyes was pride. Jennifer was finally putting the pieces together like Marco had done so many times before. The more covert, the more complicated, the more deviant things got, Marco had always understood why. He didn't care that he didn't know the answer; he was just happy Jennifer did.

Jennifer continued, "You don't make money off killing innocent people. You make money by selling *altered* people that can. The Violence Group want to sell people that have been enhanced with different skills. These *alter-bots* are using their enhanced skill sets on innocent people. The VG are testing to make sure the enhanced people can use their new alterations." She pulled her arm from around Krachy's shoulder and sat back. "That's the only explanation there is."

She tapped the top of her glass a few times with a finger and stood up.

"Gimme a minute."

Jennifer disappeared into the galley then came back with a half empty bottle. Her other hand was dripping with the ice cubes she held. She dropped the cubes in and splashed a healthy amount of the liquor over them. She took a drink.

"I couldn't get what Carol said out of my mind when I talked to her the first time on *Viper II*." She looked at Carol and smiled. Jennifer was stoned, but it didn't seem to matter.

Carol's forehead puckered, then she looked at Jennifer as recognition washed over her face.

"Categorization," she reasoned.

Jennifer nodded.

"When you said that the serial killings were all different, and that only one person was actually alone when they were killed, I couldn't stop thinking about that. You were right. That is not a successful strategy for NOT getting caught, but that is a successful strategy for categorizing what you intend to sell. The VG, or whatever group they have allowed to operate under their authority, have been physically altering people that have different skill sets. They have been turning these *alter-bots* loose on Biltmire station to test their skills before selling them. What the VG has been doing is nothing short of a dry run. Any product that is sold has to be tested and pass quality control standards. The way I was framed during the riot, and the two people Krachy rescued that disappeared, fall into the *speed* category."

Mia looked past Krachy at Jennifer.

"You mean you were framed by someone that was moving so fast that they weren't even seen when they placed a weapon in your hand to frame you? Is that what you're saying, Jennifer?"

"Yes."

"The two people I rescued were next to me one second, then a split second later, they weren't," Krachy added.

Jennifer nodded then took another pull on her drink.

"Speed, yes, it had to be," Krachy exhaled.

"Thanks, love. You believing me makes my day. Today was turning into quite the shitty one up until then." Jennifer gulped down another swallow. She hadn't forgotten about Sami, not at all.

Carol tried to make sense of Jennifer's conclusion.

"But the guy that just jumped out the shower and tried to kill you failed. I mean, I saw him and was able to stop him. He wasn't faster than me. The assassin did not possess any great speed."

Jennifer shook her head.

"He was not one of the speed categories."

Marco tightened his lips.

"No, he was one of the *stealth* categories. Right, Jen?"

Jennifer lifted her glass toward him then finished off her drink.

"How else could he have gotten on and off your ship without being seen, Marco? The assassin was not enhanced with speed. The bastard was enhanced with stealth."

"This is all very interesting," Lan observed. "But how do we stop it?"

Krachy noticed Lan said *we*.

Lan twisted a cheek seeing his look. "I told you not to get misty on me!"

Jennifer turned to Krachy happy to let him answer Lan's question.

"We go ask permission from the VG, just like you and I discussed, Lan."

Jennifer's eyes turned into icy slits of death.

"Correction, love, they are going to have to ask permission from *me*."

Marco knew where she was headed with this. His smile was not friendly.

"We have three starships at our disposal."

Jennifer pushed her empty glass away and stood up.

"Can you say, BLOCKADE?"

Her smile held no warmth.

TEN

The Violence Group had many targets Jennifer's team could disrupt as part of their blockade. Some were easy to hit, some not so easy. Jennifer decided on a course of action that could be undertaken quickly and easily as part of her wider range of destructive pursuits to bring the VG knocking on her hatch to ask permission to stay in business.

Forcing the VG's hand was a lofty goal, but given Jennifer was pretty wasted when she thought it up, that could only be expected. Her being intoxicated did not mean, however, that the plan would not work. That was yesterday. Today, Jennifer's team was going to start disrupting the VG by first hitting a few easy targets.

At the very least the VG would start taking notice in about an hour. The first two targets were on-station.

"Yes, Murphy," Carol confirmed pointing at the comp screen. "Those are the two places you and I reconnoitered yesterday before we put eyes on the Hair Raisers. The first one is the place where the stolen goods are being fenced. The second one is where Gleam is being put into the inhalers."

Murphy looked at her.

"I'm just making sure, Carol. Krachy is about to climb back into a box again and if something happens to him—"

Carol looked heavenward.

"Lan knows how to get him to both locations safely through under-deck! I told her exactly where the two locations were before she and Krachy left. Krachy won't be going any-where near the Hair Raisers' location. Lan's got this. You just need to concentrate on your part, Murphy."

"All right, 'nough said." Murphy stood up. "I've gotta go," she said as she left through the hatch.

Less than 15 minutes later, Lan asked Krachy, "You ready?"

They both stood beneath the O^2 air duct that would take Krachy to the Fencers' location from under-deck.

Krachy nodded. "Comm check, you read?" He whispered.

Lan dipped her head.

"You're good," she acknowledged into the sub-vocal mic on her throat. "I'll contact Murphy once you give me the signal that all the people in the Fencers' room are unconscious."

Krachy extended his arms over his head and grunted as he pulled himself and the small cylinder of diethyl ether gas up into the O^2 air duct. The plan called for disrupting two of the VG's on-station income streams first. The disruption would start with the group of people that were fencing stolen goods. Carol and Murphy had put eyes on the group the day before, and Lan had confirmed that the Fencers worked for the VG. As it turned out, Lan *did* know more about the VG than she had admitted to Krachy during their conversation at Holy Grounds.

Lan watched Krachy make a turn in the O^2 air duct over-head. The diethyl ether cylinder slid silently around a bend in the duct being pulled along by Krachy using a nylon belt attached to his waist. The two foot long cylinder was wrapped in a few towels secured with several loops of cloth tape. The cylinder was metal and would make way too much noise against the metal O^2 air duct walls without the towels to deaden the sound.

Krachy felt marginally better being enclosed in a metal box again after the traumatic episode with the spiders the day before. Carol assured him that he was nowhere near the Hair Raisers' location. Regardless, sweat started to dimple his fore-head as he inched his way closer to the Fencers' O^2 vent.

Drab light spilled in from the vent ahead. Krachy kept a slow but steady pace pulling himself and the cylinder through the air duct toward his target. He stopped just short and ventured a look inside. The three people in the room looked like they were going about their daily routine.

"Stand by," Krachy whispered.

"Copy that," Lan confirmed. She held her hand comp up to her mouth. "Stand by, Murphy."

Murphy acknowledged Lan's commo. Murphy was out on the main concourse street making her way toward the Fencers' location. She had on a Food Theory delivery worker uniform that she'd bought on-station the day before. She also rented a smart cart cargo vehicle just like the one Food Theory workers used to deliver food. The smart cart cargo vehicle rolled along behind Murphy mirroring her pace. She slowed, not wanting to get too close to the Fencers' location until Lan gave her the all clear to approach. The Fencers' used a back room behind a shipping container supply store.

At the air vent, Krachy pulled a transparent plasti tube out from under the shirt collar behind his neck. He shifted his body to one side of the narrow duct so he could pull the cylinder closer to attach the tube. Before Krachy attached the tube, he pulled a gas mask out of his shirt collar and put it on. The efficient half-mask was designed to protect a person from high concentrations of fumes, mists and gases. The soft, pliable plasti rubber provided a customized and pressure-free fit, conforming to his face.

After he adjusted the strap to get the half-mask snug, he attached the tube to the cylinder nipple. Then he squeezed the other end between two fingers so that it would flatten enough to be pushed through a horizontal slit in the vent. He pushed the tube through until the tip was an inch inside the room then turned on the diethyl ether gas. The only indication that the gas was flowing out of the tube was the pressure value on top of the cylinder. After a few minutes the pressure in the cylinder began to decrease as more and more gas filled the Fencers' room.

Krachy watched the gas take effect. The three people in the room became sluggish; then the woman stumbled sideways and giggled. The two men padded in the woman's direction but didn't make it to her, instead falling to their knees before pitching forward on their faces. The woman was the last one to pass out. She fell across a stack of boxes, one arm hanging over the side.

"All clear," Krachy whispered into his mask.

"Copy that," came back in his ear.

Krachy extracted the tube from the vent, unhooked the nylon cord attached to the cylinder, then pushed the cylinder with his feet down the air duct so he had enough room to pop out the vent. The vent shot out of its frame on the second shoulder butt. Krachy turned around in the air duct then let himself down into the room careful to lift his face back from the vent frame so his mask didn't get pulled off.

He hurried over to the hatch. Before he opened it he said, "Room secure, ready to open hatch."

After about 15 seconds, Lan gave him a confirm.

Krachy opened the hatch and Murphy was waiting on the other side with her half-mask already on. Murphy darted inside and the smart cart followed. Krachy closed the hatch then Murphy touched a control panel on the cart deactivating it.

Krachy locked eyes with her. His voice was muffled under the half-mask.

"Let's grab the expensive stuff," he instructed, and moved into the room selectively grabbing armfuls of delicate electronic equipment like hand comps, comp pads, and computer chip boxes. Murphy opened several of the cargo compartments on the smart cart and loaded in the booty. After five minutes Krachy was satisfied they'd stolen the highest net worth items.

Murphy closed the cargo compartments, activated the smart cart, then waited for Krachy to open the hatch.

As Krachy started to open the hatch, he looked at Murphy and said, muffled, "I'll see you in the Gleamer's room in a few minutes."

Murphy nodded and left through the open hatch followed by the quick-moving smart cart.

Back in the Fencers' room, Krachy rushed over to the air vent lying on the deck, picked it up, and tossed it into the air duct above. He jumped up and through, then put the vent grate back in place.

Krachy, Łan, and Murphy made quick work of the Gleamer's room. There were five people in that room, but like before, the diethyl ether gas did its work. The volume of the booty was significantly less given the size of the Gleam inhalers, but Krachy surmised that the net worth of the booty was much higher than what they'd taken from the Fencers' room.

***

"The only way to get the VG to ask you to stop, Jennifer," Krachy was saying in the cargo hold of Marco's ship, "is to keep hitting their sources of revenue hard."

"This is a good start." Jennifer then turned toward Murphy, "Any problems?"

Murphy shook her head.

"No, but I'm still not sure why the two places we hit didn't have guards posted on the hatches."

Mia Julie was watching Murphy open the compartments on the smart cart and unload the booty.

"No one has ever messed with their operation before. The VG probably figure no one would have the guts to interfere, so they don't post guards. Also, the two rooms were locked from the inside."

Krachy looked at Mia. His face slick with sweat.

"The VG didn't figure on someone hitting their operations from inside the rooms."

Jennifer passed Krachy a towel.

"Now that we hit the two easy targets on-station, Marco is going to meet up with Rand's ship to help with the space targets. We're heading there now." She looked at Lan. "Thanks for helping again."

Lan looked worried.

"You realize the intel I gave you on the stolen goods and Gleam is the full extent of my knowledge of VG operations, right?"

Krachy flicked a look at her.

"What?" Lan stared back at him. "You think I'm still holding out on you?"

"I didn't say that."

Lan waited.

"Thanks," he smiled, and not just for the information.

"You're pretty high maintenance. Anyone ever tell you that?" Lan asked referring to Krachy's need for backup twice in two days.

Mia noticed a box that Murphy pulled out of a compartment on the smart cart.

"Can I see that?"

Murphy handed it to her.

Mia ground her jaw.

"What, Mia?" Jennifer's eyes moved from the box to her face.

Mia was holding a black box about the size of a pack of vape sticks. A look of surprise crossed her face. She peered intently at the box and thought for a moment, taken aback. She looked up.

"It's not even sweating."

"Why would it be sweating?" Jennifer asked.

Mia's voice was edged with disbelief.

"This box has to be powered internally and insulated." She pulled a small flap on the top of the box up. "It is!"

The others moved closer staring at the little box.

"See this control panel here? The power source reads nominal." The panel was too small for the others to see. Mia held it close to her face studying it. "The internal chiller is circulating the ice-cold preservation solution of electrolytes and nutrients so that the synthetic tissue will stay preserved."

"What synthetic tissue?"

Mia looked at Jennifer.

"It says what's inside under the control panel flap. This is an accelerated molecular computer."

The others waited.

"The molecular computer inside this box produces mechanical movements in response to nerve stimuli. It acts like a switch or a motor controlling what it's connected to."

Jennifer needed details.

"What do you mean what it's connected to? You mean it controls a part of a person's body?"

"Yes, I think so. It either controls a part of the body or whatever has been implanted in the body attached to it."

"How can a little computer be advanced enough to transfer nerve impulses to an implant without a delay?" Murphy asked. "It wouldn't be practical if there was a lag between the time the nerve fired and the moment the implanted body part moved."

"It's an accelerated computer, Murphy," Mia answered. "Accelerated computers have been around for a long time. This computer separates the data-intensive parts of a program and processes them on a separate acceleration device. That allows the control functionality to be processed by the CPU. It splits the two tasks the CPU has to process. My guess is that the acceleration device is embedded in the implant placed inside the person's body. The data-intensive process is directed to the implant so that this tiny molecular computer can pass along the nerve impulse to the implant with no time lag. This little thing is a two-way funnel with no roadblocks to slow it down."

"How do you know all this?" Krachy asked.

"My father is a quantum engineer. He works with this kind of stuff."

"He's worked with synthetic tissues like this?"

"Oh no, the accelerated computer chips he's worked with are not compatible with human tissue. The chips I've heard him talk about are small but not like this one. I didn't make myself clear when I read the label." Mia glanced at the underside of the control flap. "This one says 'Accelerated Computer Tissue Quantity 1,000.'"

"There are a thousand molecular computers in that little box?"

"Must be."

Jennifer looked at Murphy.

"Are there any more of those boxes in there?"

"No, just the one."

"Us having this might stop any more implants from being put into new subjects, new people. But it won't stop the people that already have implants. This has to be incredibly expensive. Taking this is going to piss off the VG something fierce."

"What about incoming shipments?" Lan asked. "They'll just get more. The VG might have more coming in on a cargo ship right now."

Jennifer's grin was evil. "No they don't."

Lan took that in, then sucked at a tooth.

"Rand is blockading incoming cargo with his attack battle ship, isn't he?"

"He's already started, Lan. That's why we have to go help him now. His ship *Brandish* isn't big enough to handle the prisoners and cargo booty he will capture during the blockade."

Lan's eyelids arched. She turned seeing Carol come through the hatch behind her.

Carol came to a stop.

"Everything go okay?" She looked at the others.

Krachy answered, "No problems, and a part of our booty is more valuable than we could have guessed."

"You mean the Gleam?"

"No, we snagged a device we think helps control the implants. Actually, we snagged a thousand of them."

Carol looked at Jennifer.

Jennifer eyed her. "That's right, Carol. We don't have to worry about the VG taking notice. That also goes for the Food Theory cargo ship Rand has already hijacked."

Carol didn't realize that was part of the plan. Her eyes widened.

"Rand didn't blow it out of space did he?!"

"No, he didn't even fire on it. What he's doing is merely a double-dip."

Carol let out a breath. "Good, I could have friends on that cargo shi—What did you say? Double what?"

"Double-dip, Carol. When we take prisoners during the blockade that's the first dip; when we take the food to feed them, that's the second dip. Once we start taking prisoners they have to be fed. We stop the cargo ship, board it, then take the crew as prisoners. Then we take the food the prisoners need to eat during their captivity. Rand has hijacked two cargo ships so far. A member of Rand's crew boarded one Food Theory cargo ship and took over flight control. Rand also had a crew member board a second cargo ship and take over flight control on that one too. The second cargo ship was not a Food Theory ship. It was a passenger ship. Rand is waiting for us to meet up with him in space to pass off the prisoners and booty from both ships to us. Rand's ship, *Brandish*, is an attack light cruiser so *Brandish* is the punch in this blockage.

"Marco's heavy battle cruiser *Baneful* is the prison and booty vessel. *Baneful* is the largest ship we have and can easily hold all the prisoners and cargo we snag. My ship, *Viper II*," Jennifer explained, "is shadowing *Brandish* to watch their back and provide intel on new targets. *Viper II* is an Astra Class light cruiser. It's not a battleship, but it can still provide support. Not only will the VG start to get mad with what we're doing, Biltmire Station Security will too. *Viper II* will track the battle theater around *Brandish* alerting Rand of any incoming threats from the VG or Sta Sec."

Carol wasn't upset that a Food Theory transport was hit, just confused.

"How do you even know the VG have a stake in Food Theory?"

"We don't," Jennifer said. "It's an educated guess. The VG have legit businesses. It would make sense that they have at least a silent interest in Food Theory. It fits their business model perfectly—independently owned, no Biltmire oversight, and most importantly, a recurring income stream. Food is delivered every day. The VG would want a cut of that market to help finance their other endeavors. It's not sexy or exciting, but it's reliable. Either way, hijacking food helps me keep this whole blockage going. I anticipate capturing a lot more prisoners and they have to be fed. For that matter, so do we. The food your company fixes is packed in airtight vessels, so it won't spoil. We don't know how long this blockade will last, so we'll need food for a while."

Lan looked at Jennifer with something like amazement.

"Cocky fiancée, aren't you?"

ELEVEN

Rand's heavy battle ship *Brandish* yielded unexpected booty on the second cargo ship that was hit. *Baneful* met up with *Brandish* to pass off the prisoners, captured ships, and booty. Jennifer watched the second captured cargo ship come through the magnetic containment field in the launch bay on *Baneful*. The craft eased itself down on its landing gear with a scrape. After a minute, the port airlock moved aside and several prisoners were ushered out, their hands cinched behind their backs. One prisoner stood out, and even though Jennifer had never seen the man, she recognized his description from talking with Carol. Jennifer looked at Carol.

"Is that..?"

Carol's throat tightened, "Yes, that's him." Even though Bald Man was restrained, fear fluttered in her stomach remembering the torture she'd witnessed this man conduct on Biltmire Station.

***

"We have to make him remember what happened here and dread it from happening again," Jennifer reasoned as she looked at Carol and Channing just outside of the holding cell Bald Man was in.

Channing plotted, "We need to make sure we extract value from him, if he has any to offer that is. I think we can all agree that extracting that value will involve pain." He scanned both women. "Either of you have a problem with that?"

They shook their heads.

"I'll play psycho bitch." Carol looked at Jennifer. "Me playing that role will save you from all that, okay?" Anger stroked every word. The question was no question.

Jennifer felt bad pushing this chore on Carol, but with how bad her head was injured, she just didn't have it in her to play the role Carol was going to play. She dipped her head gravely.

"I'll be the smarmy-half-reason-guy, like I'm almost on Bald Man's side," Channing conspired.

"The two buckets ready?" Carol asked.

Channing nodded.

"A member of Marco's crew will watch the vid cam in the cell and bring them in. I told him when."

Carol turned to pass her hand over the scan pad, but Jennifer grabbed her wrist.

"Hey."

Carol looked at her.

"It takes bravery to do what's right. That's what I learned from Marco."

Jennifer understood what they were about to do could get to Carol.

"I know. Playing this role will help me dump some anger. Bald Man is the source of most of that anger. We might as well use that toward a good end. There's a difference between the man in that cell and me."

"There is, Carol, a *big* difference."

Carol opened the hatch. Bald Man was standing in front of the lone chair with hands plasti-tie wrapped behind his back. Channing moved past Bald Man to stand behind him. Jennifer stepped inside and stood in the corner.

Bald Man frowned. "The fuck is going on?"

Carol wound up and slapped his face. The blow left a red handprint. She shoved Bald Man into the chair. "For God's sake, somebody secure this prisoner!"

Channing pulled Bald Man's bound wrists behind the chair back then looped a tie wrap around each ankle securing them to the chair legs. When he was done he stood stoically, arms crossed, behind the chair.

Carol was not faking anger. After what she saw this man do to a poor victim with spiders and drugs, her pent up rage had jumped the fence and was on the loose.

Jennifer barked, "We can simply kill him! What'd you think?"

Carol's shoulders moved up and down trying to pull in enough air to calm her temper.

"We can do a lot worse," she spat. "I'll terrorize him, like he's terrorized others."

"Good idea, and permanently terrorized."

Bald Man snorted, "I'm oath sworn. You think this little piece o' ass can do more to me than the Violence Group? You two have led sheltered lives, haven't you?" Despite the bluster, his voice was edged with angst.

The hatch opened and Bald Man looked that way. That was a mistake. Carol slugged him in the side of the face. The chair toppled over. Bald Man howled as the deck met his cheek with a smack. When he was pulled back upright by Channing, he tried to focus on what the person had left in front of him on the deck. Another mistake. Carol hit him again, but not as hard. He jerked his scared eyes at her.

"Don't look for any help! Look at me!" She motioned with two fingers in front of her eyes daring Bald Man to look away again. He didn't. Blood percolated on Bald Man's lip and his cheek was torn open. Sweat glistened on his slick head.

Channing took a step around Bald Man and looked over his face.

"Not too bad," he observed in a tone laced with mild concern. Channing returned to his post.

"You're a dead woman," Bald Man gulped in a breath. "You can kill me and you're still a dead woman."

"You're a torturer and murderer," Jennifer accused. "I can't prove you've killed anyone, but you set loose others that have. Your profit is innocent lives." She glanced at Carol.

"I've seen the torture." Carol's eyes moved to the plasti bucket on the floor.

It took Bald Man all the will power he had not to follow her gaze to the bucket. The previous two warnings held his eyes rigid, locked on her angry face.

Bald man pulled in a breath and clinched his jaw to delay things and search for an out.

"Who are you working for?"

"Damn it! I'm tired of this waiting shit!" Carol yelled. She pulled back her arm, Jennifer slapped a laser blade in her hand, then the blade descended in a blur.

Channing caught her wrist, halting the shank just inches from Bald Man's face. He whispered in his ear. "I can only control her for so long." The sound of the humming laser blade pulled the color from Bald Man's face. He didn't dare shift his eyes from Carol. He screwed them shut instead.

Channing released her wrist. Carol straitened. When Bald Man finally opened his eyes the laser blade was no longer in her hand. The fear streaking through him kept his focus on the evil little being standing in front of him. His mouth went dry.

As if sensing his fear, Carol grabbed the bucket and tipped it forward.

"Here are some gifts from Spiderville. Enjoy!"

Panic flared in his eyes expecting a full bucket of hairy arachnids to come shooting out onto his face. Bald Man began to scream even before the cold water splashed over him. His scream stopped abruptly when his open mouth filled with water. He started choking and coughing up water between ragged gasps. Snot streamed out a nostril.

"What, your mouth still dry?" Carol didn't wait for a reply. She sloshed another brace of water in his face.

Bald Man glared up at her spitting, "You want creds? Is that it? I can arrange that."

Carol shook her head in disbelief then looked at Channing.

"How long are you going to make me wait?" She asked annoyed. Channing smiled at her out of Bald Man's line of sight, not answering on purpose.

Bald Man's eyes were jittery. "Then what, what'd you want?"

"I want you dead." Carol said to no one in particular, like she was frustrated she couldn't have her way. Finally, "Kill him," she looked at Channing.

Immediately the laser blade snapped on next to Bald Man's ear. He rose three inches, the chair leaping with him. The heat from the knife singed his skin. That smell and Bald Man's fear filled the room.

Jennifer chimed in, "Until you tell us, we will get nowhere."

Bald Man wouldn't look at Jennifer; he was too scared to shift his gaze from Carol.

Jennifer shook her head, resigned, "Then, you just have to die. Go ahead—"

"Wait!" He made sure to tell Carol.

Carol's brow knitted. She held out her hand, Channing handed her the laser blade.

Bald Man saw the satisfaction on Carol's face. His wet body went cold with dread.

Carol toyed with the switch on the handle, and flicked it on.

"You make people conform." She studied the orange épée and snapped it off.

Bald Man's eyes grew.

Carol switched it on again, fluttering it through the air in front of his face and barked.

"Why!?" Then she turned it off.

Bald Man jerked back blinking. "Okay, okay—" His voice was thick, "I was told to make them conform."

Carol thumbed the blade alight. "I already know the who." The blade went dark.

Bald Man was fighting his VG blood oath and Carol which doubled his fear.

"I'm only given enough information to do my job. I swear. It's always like that with the VG. Unquestioning loyalty, then more responsibility and trust as you move up in rank." His feverish eyes darted from Carol to the laser blade.

Carol tensed; the blade was on and trembled in her hand.

Bald Man moaned, "In order to make certain the person conforms, I identify their most terrifying fear and use it as insurance, beyond the rejection drugs. The pain of not receiving the drugs is intolerable, so I withhold them, then layer fear on top of that. It's easy—" He failed to catch the slip. His mouth snapped shut.

She admired the blade's glow, "And...?"

"I hand off the subject to my Upper. She does the rest. She knows they'll obey." Alarm caught in his jaw thinking he'd said something wrong. He spat, "I mean, all I'm responsible for is making them conform, obey. I don't turn them loose, I don't! I swear! I don't!"

"What is implanted inside the people?"

He didn't know that. This evil little being would never believe him, never!

"All I'm told to do is make them conform. I administer rejection drugs and terrify, but I never see what is put inside them. The VG compartmentalize that from me. In fact, they compartmentalize everything." Bald Man realized for the first time the VG did that so interrogations like this yielded little. The VG wanted Lowers ignorant. It was a key part of their security.

Carol wasn't buying it. "What will be rejected?"

"I told you. I don't know." When he saw her tense, he stammered, "The enhan—, the enhancement. That's it! The enhancement will be rejected."

The hatch opened again and Carol turned; as she did Bald Man felt safe enough to sneak a look. The bucket had a mesh lid. When the hatch closed, the quiet in the cell was interrupted by scratching noises coming from the bucket.

Carol kicked it with the tip of her toe a few times. The scratching increased in volume as if what was inside was agitated it couldn't get out.

Panic flared in Bald Man's eyes.

"Why were you on that cargo ship?" Carol asked then nudged the bucket. The scratching intensified. She looked at Channing. "You better move out from there." He side-stepped Bald Man and parked himself behind Carol.

Bald Man's voice was numb with terror. "Pick up, pick up!" He looked at the bucket then Carol. "The other two prisoners escaped," he sputtered fast referring to the two torture victims Krachy rescued.

"You telling me you were on your way to get more people as replacements?" She poked the bucket. The clawing sounds re-ignited.

Bald Man jerked his head up and down.

"Yes, yes, I had to! I was ordered to get more." He shrank back in the chair trying to distance himself from what was coming next.

Jennifer shook her head angrily, "He still hasn't told us."

Bald Man's eyes darted from Jennifer to Carol. "I did! I did! I just told you!"

Carol shook her head. "Nope, you didn't." She bent over grabbing the handle. Before she lifted the bucket she said, "Open the hatch, I don't wanna be in here when these things get loose." She lifted the bucket. The prickling creepies inside sounded pissed.

Channing and Jennifer backed through the open hatch into the corridor. Carol took a step back so she could jump out of the room.

"Wait! Wait!" Bald Man looked like he was going to throw up. "Give me a chance! Don't!"

Carol's eyes burned with hate. "WHERE were you going to pick up the replacements?"

Bald Man spilled it all and then some, willfully telling Carol exactly where he was headed on the cargo ship to pick up more people as replacements for the two that escaped from he and Stone-Face-Lady, Bald Man's Upper.

Carol threw the bucket past Bald Man's head. His mouth opened in a silent scream, then she slammed the handle of the laser blade against his temple. He slumped in the chair.

Carol followed Channing and Jennifer out of the cell. The hatch closed.

Jennifer looked at Carol. "You okay?"

"He's filth. I'm just thinking about all the people he's terrorized and how he finally got some." She smiled.

"Me too," Jennifer smiled back.

Marco came down the corridor stopping short.

"Did it work?" he asked. Channing went back into the cell.

Carol answered, "Yes, we know where Bald Man was headed."

Channing came back out closing the hatch behind him. He looked at Marco.

"It worked," he said referring to the object he held in his hand. He set the bucket down. "I've got to hand it to you, Marco. This thing almost pulled the piss outta that guy," he grinned.

"Obvious little notion," Marco looked down at the round rubber ball with spikes on it. "I set it on *motion-mode*." He looked at Carol.

Carol looked amused.

"When I touched the bucket it started gyrating. The harder I tapped the bucket the more it vibrated and hopped."

The round sensory dancing ball was made of rubber with about a dozen spikes encircling it. Marco had cut the rubber off the spikes to expose the metal underneath so when the thing jumped and vibrated it would scratch the walls of the plasti bucket.

Jennifer looked at Marco. "I won't ask why you have that thing on your ship."

Marco shook his head. "Don't. C'mon, then," he spoke as they followed. "You can give me the coordinates where Bald Man was headed and we'll get underway."

The four of them followed Marco to the bridge. Once Carol gave Marco the coordinates Bald Man provided, his ship changed course surging under their feet toward their target. The four of them entered the bridge's briefing room.

Lan was seated at the conference table. "Did Bald Man threaten you?" she asked Carol.

"Yep," Carol turned to Marco, "he said whether he was dead or not I'd die. How can a Lower be worth that much to the VG?"

"Doesn't matter," Marco said. "We intercepted his transmission. As soon as he threatened you, he tried to send it off."

Carol's eyes went round. "What? You knew he was an alter-bot?" She swiveled her head at Jennifer.

Jennifer shook her head. "No, we didn't know, but we were never alone in that room with Bald Man, Carol. I always have backup. I don't leave anything to chance." She looked over at Marco.

Lan looked confused too, "Leave what to chance?"

Marco paused holding a finger to an ear bud. He looked at Lan.

"My doctor just finished examining Bald Man to see if he's enhanced. He's not an alter-bot. He is not enhanced, but the guy does have a smart chip embedded in his jaw. Standard issue and can be bought on Biltmire at any number of tech shops. The chip is linked to his optic nerve. The smart chip took a vid of Carol's interrogation. He tried to transmit it off-ship. I activated my ship's electronic counter measures the second Carol stepped in the cell with him. Bald Man's transmission went nowhere." He looked at Carol. "The smack you planted on his temple deactivated the smart chip. The SC is implanted just in front of his ear. Your hit was powerful enough to knock it offline."

"A bit too late, though," Carol still looked relieved.

Jennifer agreed, "Yeah, a bit too late, but you didn't know that."

"Like I said, didn't matter," Marco said.

"...And it never will, dealing with people like you," Lan half-said to Jennifer shaking her head. "I underestimated your Short Man Hunk too."

"I wish he was here," Jennifer said.

Marco looked at her. "Krachy still has to clean up some things on-station before he leaves his job as space station director. I spoke with him earlier. The serial killings have not started back up. That's a good sign what we're doing on our end is helping. He did say that Sta Sec was holding off dismantling the VG on-station though. Sta Sec has to regroup and can't start dismantling the VG's operation until they do some relationship repair work of their own first. The riot started because people were mad that no progress had been made to stop the killings. That put Sta Sec in a very difficult position when things got out of hand. They had to pull back their response to the riot so the rioters didn't perceive them as overreacting. They arrested a lot of people but have not started wholesale investigations into the looting or damage caused during the riots. They're letting things simmer down, for lack of a better term."

"What about me?"

"They put an all-quadrant wanted bulletin out on you, Jennifer. Your charges still stand."

"Maybe I can use that to our advantage."

Marco smiled broadly, "Now, you're seeing the angles, Ship Mate Bane." He always used his pet name for her as a sign of affection.

Jennifer gathered in Carol and Lan with her devious gaze. "You two up for helping me flush out the assholes trafficking replacements for the VG to test?"

Lan stood and came around the table. "I guess I finally realize what I said to Krachy is true. Sometimes you just have to go for it." She looked at Carol.

Carol's lips curled.

"Good, give me a few minutes with Marco and I'll meet you in the ward room. I think we need to grab a bite to eat and talk through what I have in mind. Okay?"

Both women nodded and left through the hatch.

Jennifer looked at Channing, "We're going to need you to back us up, Channing."

"I figured as much. I'll meet you in the ward room too." He recognized Jennifer's need to speak with Marco alone. He knew what was paramount on her mind. He turned at the hatch.

"Murphy will want in on this."

"I want her in on this too."

Channing dipped his head and left.

Marco's look was serious, "You didn't ask Bald Man about Sami."

"I need you to do that for me, Marco."

"Get it off your chest, Jennifer. You need to have a clear head before you land on that Space Lab Bald Man was headed to. We'll be there in three hours."

"I didn't want Carol and Channing to see what I did to Bald Man either way."

"Either way?"

"If Bald Man didn't know Sami's whereabouts I would have gone ballistic on him to make sure he was telling the truth. If he did know her whereabouts, I would have still gone ballistic on him for being a part of it. Carol and Channing don't know that side of me and I'd rather not let them see it. What Carol just did to that man would have looked friendly compared to what I would have done."

"I'll find out if Bald Man knows about Sami. Leave it to me."

"Thank you, Marco."

TWELVE

Cimmerian Space Lab was appropriately named. The space lab looked dingy, dark and isolated. The swirling field of asteroids behind the small station guarded its rear flank.

The asteroid field did more than just guard the station's ass-end it seemed. Jennifer squinted looking out the front view port of the cargo ship past the space lab.

"Is that what I think it is?" She fired the fore control thrusters to bring the ship into a gentle pre-docking orbit.

"I think so." Channing was seated beside her in the cockpit. The freeze dried body and body parts were easy to see. The slow moving asteroids behind the station bumped the body debris that shared the tight gravity well with the rotating chunks of rock.

"I don't think that's a graveyard," Jennifer deduced.

"Me either, looks like a refuse dump."

"Cargo ship, state your intentions," the commo crackled. Jennifer punched the transmit key.

"My name is Jennifer Bane. I'm here to see the Chancellor. I don't have an appointment."

"What trade?" The voice on the commo asked.

"Long term income, a life, and a promise not to destroy Cimmerian," she replied.

"Big talk for a little ship," the man responded. The crescent shaped space lab had an ion cannon turret on each horn. The two turrets swiveled and locked on to Jennifer's ship.

"Check your scanner Cimmerian. I'll wait."

Marco was monitoring Jennifer's transmission and timed his fly-by accordingly. *Baneful* rocketed through space less than a kilometer behind her cargo ship at full military power. The enormous heavy battle cruiser screamed by so fast it was not visible to the naked eye against the dark backdrop of deep space.

However, the voice on the commo noticed it for sure.

"Hold orbit cargo ship!" The man's voice was shrill.

Jennifer waited.

The man cleared his throat, "Cleared to land."

"Copy Cimmerian, thank you."

There was barely any light illuminating the small docking bay. The fore lamps on Jennifer's ship allowed her to adjust the landing through the magnetic containment field and guide the ship to rest in the bay. No one met her in the bay as she exited the airlock with her entourage. Channing stayed on-board with *the life*. Bald Man was *the life* Jennifer intended to use as part of her plan.

Murphy, Carol, and Lan followed Jennifer to the blast hatch. Jennifer looked up into the vid cam perched above the hatch. The red glow encircling the vid camera indicated infrared or night-vision. Which one really didn't matter.

The hatch moved aside.

Dim lights splashed up the V-shaped corridor walls in front of them. A narrow catwalk grating walkway was suspended down the center of the V. The up lights were positioned below the trophies on each wall of the corridor highlighting the grisly decorations.

The hatch at the far end of the corridor opened and a man stepped through.

"This way," he motioned.

The four women walked hesitantly down the catwalk grate studying the trophies to either side. They stopped in front of the man.

"I see you like the cranial and body part remains. I gathered them over quite a long period of time. I do hope you have a new one to add to my collection." His smile was forced, like he didn't have practice with it.

Jennifer overlooked his disturbing request.

"What you do with *the life* I intend to trade is up to you." She didn't want to touch the man but extended her hand anyway.

The way the man looked down at her skin was ghoulish.

"You are 33 years old, are you not?" He pulled her hand toward his eyes to study it.

She submitted to the inspection with inward revulsion. This was the price of admission.

The man released her hand and looked into her eyes. Jennifer fought her apprehension. He had an intermittent exotropia, or wandering eye. The left eye had a pronounced deviation that was focused on her breasts.

"I am 33 years old. With me is my accountant and two body guards. Of course, I know I won't need the guards. You seem like a gentleman. Am I right about that?"

The man turned to look at Murphy, Carol and Lan for the first time, but quickly turned back to Jennifer surveying her body with his creepy leer.

"You have been busy near Biltmire executing your destructive blockage." The growing bulge in his groin was unmistakable. "Would you allow me to pay you now for the use of your body—upon death?" The calm delivery of his request was more disturbing than the question.

"You like my whole package, Chancellor. Since you know I've been busy, you also know that I am a person of my word. My word to you is, *NO*."

The brooding dark-haired Chancellor stared at her. He turned expecting them to follow.

Jennifer turned to her friends and hissed softly, "Back to the ship and leave."

The instant she stepped past the hatch threshold it snapped shut behind her leaving the three women staring at the closed hatch.

Murphy turned, grabbed both women by an elbow, and yanked them down the catwalk and through the blast hatch. Channing shoved Bald Man, *the life*, out the airlock of the cargo ship and waved the three women to hurry. He had been listening via the sub vocal mic on Jennifer's throat.

Carol tried to protest but as soon as she opened her mouth Channing clamped a hand over it and forced her into the airlock behind Lan and Murphy. He jumped into the pilot seat, fired up the engine, and eased the ship out of the bay.

The monocle the Chancellor slipped over his wandering eye was more than a lens to correct visual perception. This one was thick and looked like it enhanced the distance his eye could see. When he turned to look at Jennifer before he sat down, his eyeball was large in the round loupe.

"Please take a seat, and tell me how you managed your impediment to Biltmire so swiftly."

They both took a seat on a low couch against the bulkhead. Jennifer sat as far away from the Chancellor as possible. There were shifting figures around the room in darkened corners, but the light was so low she couldn't see the people clearly.

She could not see his face very well as he got comfortable on the far end of the couch but felt his monocular penetrate the darkness to study her.

"You don't sound upset," Jennifer observed.

"Why would I be upset? The arrangement I have with the VG is short term."

"I see." Jennifer didn't flinch when a short woman appeared at her side holding a tray with drinks on it. Her eyes locked on the woman's face, but the servant's eye sockets held no eyeballs. Both eyelids were stitched closed.

"No, thank you." Jennifer had no intention of putting anything from this place in her body.

The servant shuffled toward the Chancellor. He grabbed a tumbler and drank all the liquid then burped. He took the one

Jennifer refused and rested it in his lap. The woman drifted out of sight like fog, gone.

"You protected your friends. You reveled a weakness then."

"Yes, I care for people. If I didn't, I would have destroyed your space lab before I landed."

"Oh!" He licked his lips. The front third of his tongue was cut down the center revealing a forked tongue. "You care if I die. How civil!"

"Not civil, practical, Chancellor. There will always be operations like yours providing human raw materials. I destroy one, another one pops up in its place. You are a practical part of the space trade."

"Based on your landing clearance comm, you seem to want to help me, and allow me to prosper. Why?"

"My aim is on the VG. You know what I've started and where it will lead. I want to slice off the arm of trade that you're doing with the VG. I'm willing to explain, but I can't take a lot more time doing it. There is a time factor involved. A person that is very important to me has gone missing. Her time being safe and retrievable is limited. The *life* I dropped off in your docking bay does not know where she is. I checked..." Jennifer explained referring to Bald Man.

The Chancellor straitened, intrigued.

"Do tell me how you checked?" His sick anticipation of gruesome details was clearly articulated with each word.

"That is minor. The man is minor. I offer him to you as a sign of my willingness to negotiate."

"He is not *you*. *You* are worth so much more."

"I've already told you, no. Must you treat this conversation like a barter exchange in the market? I have serious business to discuss."

He exhaled loudly. "All right, if we must."

"Will you consider an offer to stop trafficking human replacements to the VG for them to test?"

"I don't know what the VG does with the bodies once they pay me for them, other than they upgrade or enhance them somehow."

"Is that a no?"

The Chancellor hesitated trying to extend the conversation with Jennifer by mistake.

"That is a *maybe*."

Jennifer suppressed a sigh—the Chancellor's attempt to extend the conversation was a big mistake indeed.

"I will now turn your maybe into a yes. Listen carefully, as I will not repeat myself." She stood up then took two strides toward the Chancellor plopping herself down on the couch next to him.

"First, remove the tumbler from your lap. I've seen a hard-on before." She looked down at his crotch, then back into his wandering eye, the pupil of which dilated.

He did as she asked, but had no false illusion that she was getting ready to give him a handy. Not with the hateful look in her eyes. He swallowed as he pulled the tumbler from his crotch and set it on a table next to the arm of the couch.

Jennifer's eyes were wild with anger.

"I am not afraid of you, little man. I was only afraid of what you would have done to my friends, but you made the mistake of letting me remove them from the equation. I'm very surprised that you didn't know how dangerous I was given what I've accomplished blockading Biltmire over the past few days. And if you don't control that wandering eye of yours from staring at my chest, I will snatch the other eye out of its socket and have it put in your blind servant's head."

The Chancellor snapped the eye back to her face. He *could* control the wandering eye, given the right incentive.

"I came here in good faith."

The Chancellor's scalp prickled. He reached up with a hand to scratch it. He stammered.

"I can—, I can bargain in good faith."

"That time has past." Jennifer looked around the room lazily. "You've pulled the drive out of your people, Chancellor. They don't seem to want to protect you." She locked eyes with him. "I guessed as much. They're as sick of your perverted shit as I am and I just met you." She glanced down not finding a bulge any longer. "You're just a creepy little man that carves up people and sells their flesh. On second thought, I am not going to try to turn your maybe into a yes." She stood up to leave.

"Wait!"

It took all the energy Jennifer had to stop her arm from unloading a fist to the side of his face. She knew she could hate, but this was beyond that. Instead she looked around the room.

"Those of you who want to live follow me now."

The people in the room limped, shuffled, and lurched from the shadows hindered by the particular deformity they suffered from. They moved toward her in different states of confused obedience, not hurrying per se, just willing to follow someone else, *anyone* else, but the Chancellor.

The Chancellor's reaction time was pitiful. He tried to reach for a weapon in a hidden compartment on the couch arm. Jennifer dropped her backside down onto the hinged lid as he made a grab for it. He screamed until she jerked her knee up into his nose with a crunch. His head snapped back, unconscious.

"Channing, land again. I need some help, change of plans."

Jennifer's head didn't hurt very bad from the ordeal. The meds she took before she landed smoothed out her tension as did using her knee instead of her fist to settle things.

Channing confirmed in her ear bud. Once he did, she started to look over her human cargo. What she saw turned her stomach, but she gritted her teeth and started helping the infirmed people toward the docking bay where Channing would land the cargo ship soon. The blind woman was the first person she helped. None of the unfortunates spoke; they just followed and gathered in the landing bay to wait for reprieve. The people wanted a chance for life, any life other than the one they were going to leave behind on this hellish asylum.

Once all the injured people were extracted, Jennifer ended the chance of Cimmerian Space Lab ever harming another person. *Baneful* sent a devastating volley of missiles into the station. The explosion made no sound in space. With no oxygen, the flash of impact was quick. Cimmerian Space Lab blinked out of existence, the universe now a better place without it, and without the evil person running it.

Jennifer turned to Carol, "That felt good." She smiled as the two of them left *Baneful's* bridge heading for the lift tube.

"I was so mad at you when you made us leave the space lab, Jennifer."

"Still mad?"

"That is such a dumb question."

The lift tube arrived; the hatch opened and they entered. Carol looked up at Jennifer.

"You didn't press the Chancellor for Sami's location. Why?"

The lift tube stopped. They stepped out and strode down the corridor toward the landing bay. Jennifer didn't answer.

Carol pulled Jennifer to a halt. "Give," she insisted.

Jennifer's face was solemn. "He may have wanted his life in exchange. Besides, we can just ask one of the people we rescued if Sami was ever there."

"I don't know how to say this without sounding like an uppity big sister, but…I'm proud of what you just did."

"Thanks, I'm proud too, of what all of us just did. That's saying a lot considering we just killed a man."

The hatch to the landing bay opened. The activity inside was measured and orderly. The two captured cargo ships rested in the landing bay with the prisoners, and the rescued people from Cimmerian dispersed throughout the open deck space around the ships. It was meal time. Food was being brought down the Food Theory cargo ship ramp and handed out. Mia Julie shouted orders to the crew members handing out the chow and to the people waiting to be fed. Six guards lined the periphery of the landing bay, their flechette rifles braced and ready.

Lan was helping pass out the food, as was Murphy. Channing stood next to Mia as personal security. Bald Man was one of the prisoners lining up to receive food.

"Bald Man looks pretty tame," Carol observed. He looked like a shadowy reflection of his old, confident self.

"He does. I don't think he'll be giving us much more trouble. Hell, after what you did to him, he may quit the VG once this is all over."

Jennifer watched the activity in the hold with something like satisfaction. The woman servant with no eyes was being led to some deck space to sit and eat. A tray of food was handed to her. Watching the blind lady made Jennifer regret not snatching the Chancellor's eye to put it to some good use.

"We still accomplished what we set out to do with Bald Man's intel. We shut down the pipeline of replacement human test subjects being shipped to the VG. The VG's supply chain is drying up. *Brandish* and *Viper II* are still on the hunt disrupting in-coming and out-going shipping around Biltmire. The blockage has only been active for two days, but we're already making a difference," she glanced at the blind woman, then back at Carol, "in many ways."

Carol watched Jennifer make her way over to where the blind woman was seated, kneel down next to her, and rest a hand on her shoulder. The woman was pulling a fork of food to her mouth and stopped to listen to Jennifer talk into her ear. The fork of food drifted down onto the tray as the blind woman listened. No emotion painted the blind woman's face until she opened her mouth to say something and smiled. Jennifer squeezed the blind woman's shoulder briefly, stood up, then came back over to where Carol was standing.

"Her name is Aretha."

"Pretty name."

"Pretty lady," Jennifer's head swiveled at the touch on her shoulder.

Marco had come through the hatch. "A tight beam trans came in for you." He jerked his head to follow.

Jennifer left through the hatch with Marco. Carol trailed behind them as they made their way to the conference room just off the bridge.

Jennifer reached down to the recessed keypad on the table accepting the vid feed. The large vid screen on the far bulkhead wall snapped on. Sami's bruised face appeared in the display. Her eyes were bloodshot and submissive. After just 10 seconds, which seemed like an eternity, a woman yanked Sami by the shirt out of camera view and sat in the chair she'd pulled Sami from. It was Stone-Face-Lady, the solemn-faced bitch that Carol had seen torture the terrified woman back on Biltmire Space Station. She opened her mouth to speak.

—Jennifer cut the feed. The vid screen blinked off.

Marco fixed his troubled gaze on Jennifer.

"I know that was tough."

Jennifer clinched her eyes shut then opened them.

"It was," she stepped back from the table then left through the hatch.

Carol stood staring at Marco dumbfounded.

"She had to do that, Carol. She had no choice," Marco reasoned.

Carol blinked.

"The VG was going to threaten Sami's life if Jennifer didn't stop the blockage. Jennifer had to make it clear that didn't matter to her."

"…Even though it does matter to her. It matters very much to her." Carol pulled out a chair and sat down shakily.

"Jennifer has to make them understand nothing will stop her. Snapping the vid feed off lets the VG know nothing they do will stop her—nothing! Just like the dread you planted in Bald Man when you interrogated him, the VG have to dread what will happen next. The only way to reinforce that was to do what Jennifer just did."

"But you could have done what she just did, Marco!" Carol's words came out in a rush. "You could have snapped the vid comm off to save her from all that hurt."

"No, I couldn't. The VG have targeted Jennifer from the very start. They had to see that Jennifer is just as dangerous as they thought. Any other response would have been a huge mistake." Marco plastered a smile on his face.

Carol didn't understand why. Then she did.

"—That's right, Carol. If the VG dare kill Sami, they now know what will happen to them too."

THIRTEEN

Jennifer couldn't scrub her skin hard enough. She was frantic to get the Chancellor's stink off her body. She used a washrag on her hand. He had touched her there. She remembered that her knee had connected with his nose, so she cleaned that too, even though skin never made contact. She realized she was going through the motions of taking a shower to forget the look on Sami's face when the vid screen blinked off—it was awful. And she was awful for leaving her. She'd abandoned her friend.

"Jennifer," Carol was there as Jennifer stepped from the shower.

Jennifer's eyes widened with alarm. "Carol!"

"I've never waited for someone to finish a guilt-stricken shower before," Carol smirked. She and Aretha sat on the rack in Jennifer's cabin.

Jennifer started to dry herself.

"You're so damn self-assured. You really do think you're my big sister, don't you?" She huffed.

"Get over yourself." Carol turned to Aretha. "She's always like this. Maybe you can do something with her." She got up and left through the hatch.

Aretha lifted her nose, "I haven't smelled fresh like that in a while."

Jennifer looked at her while wiping her legs.

"I couldn't wait to get the Chancellor's stink off me. You want to…?"

"…Take a shower? No," she shook her head, "Already did, thanks."

Jennifer put on her flight suit and ran a brush through her hair. "The food suit you?"

"Pretty good, yeah," Aretha covered a burp with her hand. "Carol said she works on Food Theory. She's an interesting lady."

"And arrogant, the little shi—" Jennifer cut off the retort.

A huge smile lit up Aretha's face.

"What?" Jennifer sat down at the comp desk.

"The by-play between you two is a refreshing change for me."

"Would you believe I just met her?"

"Not surprised. You make friends fast."

Jennifer studied her. Aretha was in her forties and kept herself in excellent shape at five-feet-one and a-hundred-twenty pounds, most of it muscle. She had on some ship-board grays she'd been given that fit her surprisingly well.

"My fitness is part of my dream."

Jennifer didn't understand the statement, or how Aretha knew what she was thinking.

"I've dreamed of having a life after Cimmerian. I've thrown every idle minute I've had into it." She pulled herself up into the rack, and leaned against the bulkhead getting comfortable.

"Do you want me to separate Bald Man from the rest of you from Cimmerian?" Jennifer offered.

"No," Aretha said off-handed. "Bald Man's not a threat. He's not the one that took my eyes. He's only the courier that delivered them."

"I didn't know that. I'm sorry."

Aretha tilted her head like she was studying Jennifer with a gaze she didn't possess.

"You didn't know a lot of things, but you sure made up your mind in a hurry. I heard you talk about your friend to the Chancellor. Carol said her name is Sami, but she was never on the space lab, at least not in the last month."

Jennifer's guilt over abandoning Sami turned to anger.

"I hate that I know how to deal with people like the VG, but they only understand one thing. What got me to that realization, that decision, was a series of personal events in my life that were negative. I want to turn them into a positive. I had to abandon Sami to get down that road."

"I've just been trying to survive, then fate intervened. You're a reminder that where we start out and where we end up are out of our control."

"What are you saying?"

"You gotta roll with the punches and keep an open and positive mindset to everything, just that simple."

"Carol is crafty…" Jennifer looked suspicious. "She put you up to this?" Referring to Aretha's knack for helping guilt-stricken people.

"No, I told Carol I want to help."

Jennifer swallowed, certain she did not want to pull anyone else into this mess.

Aretha's other senses were peaked. She heard it.

"I can't go back in time. My eyes are gone. That doesn't mean the rest of me doesn't work. Let me help."

"No."

"Then let me try to get my sight back."

"That's not fair. I can't say no to that. Don't put me in that position, please."

Aretha scooted forward on the rack, penetrating Jennifer with her non-stare.

"I thought I had a look that could burn skin." Jennifer shuddered.

"I like being treated like a whole person. I am glaring at you. I'm very pissed off and want to help. Let me."

"I will let you help with something."

"What?"

"Why was it so easy for me to take over that space lab? There were no guards and the people in the room were passive, although I could see why they were."

"The Chancellor never left a ship in the docking bay, ever. I've only been there a month, but there has never been a ship docked that any of us could hijack. The next source of oxygen is a three-hour flight in any direction. Space was our prison, but there have been guards. Up until yesterday, there were four guards. Then a ship came and they all left on it."

"That's about the same time we started blockading Biltmire Space Station."

"It's not a coincidence. In the short time since I lost my eyes, my ears have taken up the slack. In fact, all my senses are heightened. I heard what the guards were talking about before they left. They made a deliberate effort to keep their conversation private, but I heard what they said."

Jennifer waited.

"Aren't you going to tell me?"

"No."

"Why not?"

"You aren't *really* going let me help, that's why."

Jennifer rolled her eyes. She couldn't believe this woman's gall.

"I can hear your breath pick up, Jennifer. You have a short fuse."

"Are all the women I'm going to meet on this thing going to have an attitude? I don't need your information then. If it means putting you in the line of fire, hell no, I don't need your intel!"

"That must have been hard to say given I'm disabled."

Jennifer opened her mouth then clamped it shut like a fish.

"I'm new at playing the disabled card. You like?"

Jennifer wanted to smack the smug look off Aretha's face, then felt guilt-stricken again about that. Her head started to hurt. She grabbed the bottle of meds on the desk and dry swallowed two pills.

"That sounded chalky," Aretha taunted.

Jennifer's face went ashen.

"You can't win this. I'll just keep pushing your buttons. How about this—I owe you one. Please let me help. That make you feel better about it?"

"No."

"Too bad. That's about all I have left."

"Somehow, I doubt that, Aretha."

"You should. I'm a part of this. You may as well accept that. I do, and it's not a card I'm playing. I live in darkness and sleep's not an escape." Her body was taught with outrage. Her muscles rippled with it.

Jennifer's eyes shot open shocked that Aretha extended her hand at the same time Jennifer did to shake. They shook.

"Deal," Jennifer sighed. "Can I ask you to at least follow my lead when GO time comes?"

"Of course."

Jennifer went into the head and got a cup of water. She sat back down swallowing some.

"Good, tell me more."

"The guards were told to provide 'protection detail on client,' quote un-quote."

Jennifer went white. Why she understood what that meant was unclear, but she did.

"They're shutting things down! They're consolidating forces and cutting their losses. It has to be!" She jumped up, "Grab my arm—We have to go!"

Aretha extended a hand that Jennifer pushed onto her bicep. Aretha was pulled along down the corridor then into the lift tube. Jennifer grabbed the hand comp from her pocket as the lift tube went up to the bridge.

"Murphy…" she waited for a response. As she did, the lift tube opened and Jennifer guided Aretha onto the bridge then into the conference room.

"Jennifer?" Murphy answered.

"Get Carol and Lan and meet me in the bridge conference room, now!"

"Copy that," came the reply.

Marco stepped through the briefing room hatch with a puzzled look on his face.

Jennifer guided Aretha to a chair then looked at him.

"Can you pull up the tight beam vid trans from the VG again?"

Marco nodded and moved to the recessed keypad on the table. He pecked in some commands. As he did, Murphy, Carol and Lan came through the hatch.

Jennifer gathered the women in with her eyes.

"I'll explain more in a minute, but I need you to help Aretha and I. Take a seat," she instructed. They did.

Marco brought up the tight beam vid trans to the first frame. Sami's helpless stare filled the large view screen on the bulkhead.

Jennifer sat next to Aretha and placed a hand on her forearm.

"Aretha, I need you to listen carefully. Marco is going to play a vid trans start to finish. My friend Sami is framed in the display in an unknown room." She looked at Murphy, "Murphy can you EQ the sound feed on it?"

Murphy nodded and pulled out her hand comp touching the screen. The glow from the small screen lit up her face as she fingered the display then looked up.

"I pulled up Sound EQ. It's a basic equalizer app. When Marco plays the vid trans through once, I'll capture it digitally. The app only has a 9-band equalizer, but it's all I have on my HC."

Aretha spoke up, "That might be enough. I think I know where Jennifer is headed with this."

Lan snorted, "Good, 'cause I don't."

Jennifer explained, "I want us to analyze the vid trans and see if we can identify where Sami is being held."

Lan looked side-long at Carol. Her brow drew down, then she turned to Jennifer.

"I get it, now. You want Carol and I to study the room Sami's in to see if we can identify the location."

Jennifer's jaw tightened, the muscles clinched. She nodded.

Marco made a full pass of the vid feed. Murphy captured the feed digitally on her HC. Then Marco started the vid again. The vid feed played through a dozen more times. The more it repeated, the more familiar Aretha got with it.

Aretha inched forward in her chair tilting her face at the screen. On what had to be the twentieth playback she called out, "There!" She turned to Murphy, "Can you isolate that piece of the feed and play it back?"

Marco stopped the playback and waited for Murphy.

"Yes, I'll pipe it through the room speakers." She pecked at the screen. "Okay, here it is at regular speed."

Murphy let the sound bite play repeatedly. It was only two seconds of video sound filled mainly with white noise. The others in the room concentrated but couldn't pull out anything from the background noise that was identifiable.

Aretha instructed, "Pull down the mid-range, the white noise, pull it all the way out if you can."

Murphy tried. Since no one spoke on the vid, there seemed to be no discernible difference in the sound. The light static of the vid trans receded. Murphy played the two second snippet in a loop over and over.

While Aretha studied the sound, Carol and Lan studied the room. Problem was, they didn't recognize it. A nondescript wall was behind Sami with no features on it to make it distinct.

"Increase the treble, more high-end," Aretha instructed.

Murphy complied as best she could. The repetitive recording had a sound variation. It was faint but clear. Not clear to the others, but that didn't matter. Aretha started to hear it.

The loop played for Aretha another few minutes, then, "Pull up the sub-bass a little." She listened as it played several times. "More volume!"

Murphy cranked it up. The variation was faint but it repeated so many times it started to become clear what the sound was. There were two faint words, but they were so familiar, so distinct, there seemed to be no doubt.

"Prisna tahfr, prisna tahfr, prisna tahfr, prisna tahfr."

Jennifer's eyes blazed with hate. "Prisoner transfer. Sami's being held in Biltmire detention."

The statement was ominous, the consequences, the meaning even more so. But Jennifer only saw the angle. The next step that had to be accomplished. She looked at Marco.

"The VG is shutting things down and that means anyone on-station that could alter their plan will be killed."

Marco jumped up running out the hatch. The orders he shouted to change course and head for Biltmire were loud out on the bridge. The women in the room grabbed the table leaning with the abrupt course change of the huge battleship.

Carol's defiant words masked her fear.

"But they aren't going to kill Sami, Jennifer. They know what you'd do to them if they did!"

"That's right. They won't kill her *because* I know they have her, but they can have Krachy killed. They don't know we found out where Sami is being held. So, if Krachy is killed, alone, by himself, with no one to see it, he'll be considered just another serial killer victim."

Carol looked at Lan, the two women unified in what had to be done next. Their help *might* be needed after all. Once on-station, they could help plan a route to Krachy's apartment from under-deck.

***

At night, when the shops closed down, Krachy walked through a near silent space station. His day was finally over. He was heading back to his apartment after a series of long meetings when he felt a pinch of emotion—fear.

This feeling was not the bold, crawl across your face, nibble-your-flesh-terror he experienced when he was trapped in the box with the spiders. This was a shiver of voyeurism, as though he was being watched. He turned fast, startled because he sensed that someone was behind him on the balcony leading to his flat. But there wasn't—nothing. It was after 1am station time, eerily silent.

Why was Krachy panting? He didn't know, but he stepped over to the third floor balcony railing to look down. A few people were going about their business below on the concourse street. Nothing out of the ordinary, but then his eyes caught movement. Two hands gripped the second floor balcony railing below then were gone. He swung back around and caught a faint whisper of a movement, as if in the fraction of a second he decided to turn the person behind him withdrew from his sight path.

How could Krachy have missed seeing a person if the person was there? That same person could not have just been on the second floor then behind him, could they? His flat was close, the hatch visible just down the balcony. He could not command his legs to move from the safety of the railing. With his back to the railing no one could be behind him. There was just open air behind his shoulders. Krachy's head swiveled. The only interruptions on the balcony were columns that supported the balcony. The balcony railing was anchored into each uniformly spaced pillar. Could a person hide behind the support pillars? Of course they could. Adrenaline surged through him. He felt trapped, yet no one, nothing was visible to indicate danger—not a thing.

Krachy looked toward his flat again and thought to himself: *Rule number one, Don't let your imagination get the best of you.* His head turned and in the brief instant he'd shifted his gaze a SeeHead appeared on the deck in front of him. The communication display looked out of place. Krachy had used them hundreds of times. The SeeHead was a video conferencing tool. It was a standalone device designed to represent a remote person physically in a meeting room. Facial features were embodied by the high-def display forming a head shape.

The SeeHead spoke to Krachy. "We should meet," the man's face said.

"I don't know you."

"Your friend Lan told you who I was, Ser Bantor." The robotic device mimicked the head movements of the man in crystal-clear detail.

"Parent."

"Yes, I am the parent of the VG. I want to make amends for the failings of one of my children." Parent's eyes squinted. "Trustwords."

"There are enhanced people stalking me. Why?"

"The two people asked to help. The man and the woman you rescued from my disobedient child wanted to help."

Krachy blinked and a woman stood motionless beside the pillar to his left. Krachy turned to the right and a man stood next to that pillar. They were the two people he saved from Stone-Face-Lady and Bald Man.

Preoccupied, Krachy didn't hear Parent's second request. Then Parent repeated it.

"We should meet. Your new friends won't harm you."

The man and woman took a step toward Krachy. The woman spoke.

"Will you come with us? Parent will not hurt you. Neither will we." Her smile had a hint of what seemed like regret; however, it looked warm and genuine.

Krachy tensed realizing what these people were capable of.

"Why should I believe you? You've been responsible for killing 15 people."

Parent answered.

"That's just it, Ser Bantor. The VG have not killed anyone. A disobedient child is responsible. Help me stop her. I want to work with you, alongside you."

Krachy considered the truth in that last statement but wasn't convinced. Trust was not easy to give to someone that knew about the killings.

"You've waited too long to contact me. You could have helped stop the loss of innocent lives if you'd come to me sooner. I don't think I want to work with a person like that. In fact, I know I don't."

Parent shook his robotic head. A line appeared between his brow.

"I've made mistakes. I *have* waited too long. But waiting any longer will have more serious consequences than the 15 innocent lives lost, much, much, more. We should meet, now."

Krachy would never forgive himself if he missed the chance to save lives. He tried a new way to convince himself. Krachy addressed the woman.

"I worked to save your life, but you ran away from me." He turned to the man, "You too, you both ran away. I risked everything to get you both out. Bald Man sprung a spider trap that almost worked." Despite himself, renewed dread pulsed through Krachy at the thought of the spiders succeeding in their fang-fueled rampage on his flesh.

The man gulped. His mouth moved but no words came out. In electric fast movement, the woman darted like lightning to the man's side. One moment she was standing near the pillar, the next wisp of light-shifting blur she was not. She stood next to the man, her arm wrapped around his shoulder, comforting him.

Krachy realized the man was frightened about the same thing he was—spiders. The man's face was wild with terror, but he was able to control himself long enough to speak.

"I'm sworn to my Parent. My first impulse was to go to him."

The woman pulled her arm from the man and looked at Krachy.

"He's my husband, but we are both oath sworn to Parent. When I woke up in the cable-way after you rescued me, my only thought was to be with Parent."

Krachy needed to know. "Did you or your husband kill innocent people?"

The question looked like it made the blood go cold inside the woman's veins.

"No!" She shouted. "We did not conform to that. You rescued us just in time!" She looked down at the SeeHead. "I wanted to help him, Parent, but I'm not sure about that any longer." She peered at Krachy. "Thank you for getting us out, but you're not the man I wanted you to be. I've endured enough pain. You're making it worse by accusing me of murder. You have no idea how close we were to conforming, but we didn't, wouldn't!"

If the woman was lying she was good at it, very good.

"I had to know. You have abilities that no one has ever seen. You have to know that. You have to know I would have thought you were a part of it all."

"I do know that. But what you don't know will be explained by Parent. Meet him, please."

Krachy was at a crossroad. His instincts told him this was the opportunity to end the misery, the killings, and re-build something good from it all. He did not want to have to forgive himself for not helping, not doing the right thing. He realized it was his responsibility. He needed to stop the killings if he could.

"I will meet with him."

The man swallowed, gaining back some color in his face, but there was more to his foreboding look, much more.

"We also came here to warn you."

Krachy shivered involuntarily. The hands on the second floor! He didn't hesitate, twisted at the waist, and jumped the railing flinging himself over the balcony. His grip on the top railing was strong as he floated out into the air then shot his other hand to the bottom railing to catch his weight. He grunted and looked down, searching. There, on the railing on the second floor balcony eight feet below, the two hands of a person. He let go and dropped.

Krachy's feet landed on one of the man's hands. On impact his knees bent to vault himself over the man and onto the deck with a tuck and roll. Up on his feet, Krachy's legs started pumping hard with no look back. He must have stunned the man which gave him a brief head start. He knew he couldn't escape the two Speed-People he'd just talked to on the third floor. But that was not what he was running from. He had sensed Stealth-Man watching him from the second floor. It had to be him! As soon as Speed-Man said, "We also came to warn you," Krachy acted, like he had always acted, when he sensed danger.

Krachy's eyes landed on a hallway up ahead between two shops. He juked hard and darted into the narrow hall barely wide enough for his shoulders.

Stealth-Man shook off the pain in his hand and followed. He was the same assassin that tried to kill Jennifer aboard Marco's ship with the garrote.

Stealth-Man had been waiting on the second floor knowing that Krachy would be coming back to his flat on the third floor sometime that night. Then the assassin would have made his move.

Stealth-Man was not unusually fast but that didn't matter now. He saw Krachy sprint into the narrow passageway and grinned. He knew corridors like that ran the length of each shop on either side of it. He ran after Krachy into the hallway knowing what he would see. He would see Krachy running away from him in the close confines of the hallway. Stealth-Man pulled the laser pistol out of the holster ready to end Krachy's life, the pain in his hand where Krachy landed on it a vague annoyance.

Stealth-Man entered the narrow passageway and froze. Krachy was not in the corridor. How could that be? Stealth-Man had entered right after Krachy did. There was no way Krachy could be that fast. The hall was over 40 meters long.

A crushing weight slammed down onto Stealth-Man's head. Neck vertebrae compressed rifling a jolt of searing pain through his spine. Stealth-Man crumpled to the deck with a shudder under Krachy's diving double knee drop from above. Krachy had scurried up the narrow alley walls ambushing Stealth-Man from above, turning the assassin into prey.

Stunned, Stealth-Man could not feel his legs, but his eyes worked. What he saw was the blind madness of a man that was going to end his life. Before Stealth-Man could feel the fear that unmanned his living self, Krachy came for his soul. Krachy was now the assassin. Years of battle-skill propelled his powerful forearms around the neck of his assailant. Krachy lifted the stunned man up, tucking his head and neck next to the man's head before whipping the man through the air back-wards using the full weight of the upside-down body as lever-age. The muscle buster was an incredibly dangerous move, and this incident proved how deadly it could be. Krachy arched backward slamming the man back-first through the air to the deck. The impact shockwave snapped the man's spinal cord with a wet crunch.

Krachy stood. His shoulders touched the sides of the narrow alley coffin he had just made, looking down as the last exhale of life escaped from Stealth-Man's mouth.

FOURTEEN

Krachy's head sprung around at the touch on his shoulder. By reflex he shot a hand out to grab the wrist of Speed-Woman. Still breathing hard, Krachy yelled.

"Tell me you didn't set me up! Tell me!" The command was loud in the tight confines of the alley.

Speed-Woman shook her head.

"I did not set you up." She glanced down at the dead body then back into Krachy's eyes. "That man was not loyal to Parent. We should go, to meet Parent before Station Security intervenes and the opportunity to end all this is gone."

Krachy was pulled out of the hallway so fast he did not know what was happening until he felt the cool wind on his face. The view to either side of Krachy blurred, like he was in a tunnel, but the tunnel was bright. The air across Krachy's face pushed at his cheeks rippling his skin. His eyes began to water. The wind pushed against his body, like he was falling straight down, close to terminal velocity. But the scene to either side was horizontal. He was not falling. He was being carried through the space station, the gravity of shifting turns in the corridors jolting his head. He grunted and tensed his neck to keep his head from being snapped sideways in pain. Then it stopped. Tears streamed over his face from blinking eyes. Krachy was in front of a hatch that opened.

The face Krachy had spoken to on the SeeHead looked back at him. Parent was a thin, tall, black man, with a narrow, angular face, and a small scar laced into one eyebrow. Krachy watched Parent's dark brown eyes which were concerned but confident.

"Come in, Ser Bantor. Here, take this and wipe your eyes." Parent held out a few tissues.

Krachy gulped air as though he had been underwater. He glanced side-to-side seeing Speed-Man and Woman for the first time. They released Krachy from their grasp.

Speed-Man grabbed the tissues. "Go ahead, wipe your eyes."

Dazed, Krachy reached for the tissues and wiped his eyes and face. He was speechless, but he was also irritated that he failed to control the situation being brought here by force.

Parent guided Krachy in through the hatch by an arm. The adrenaline from killing Stealth-Man coupled with the unreal journey pulled strength from Krachy's legs. He stumbled, caught his weight with an outstretched hand on a chair-back, then righted himself. He scanned the troubled look on Parent's face and realized these people could have made short work of him given their scary abilities. Krachy exhaled pounds of hard tension. He was not in danger. Maybe these people did want to end the misery. He sat down before he fell down. This was no act, no ploy. He was weak with disorientation. A cup of coffee and a croissan'wich was placed on the table in front of him. The gesture was eerily similar to what Lan Chevron did for him at Holy Grounds.

Parent pulled out a chair at the table and dipped his head at the food.

"You should eat a little. It'll calm you down."

Krachy pulled the croissan'wich to his mouth, hesitated, and turned his head to find Speed-Woman and Man behind him on either side of the hatch. He turned his attention back to his food, took a few ravenous bites, then washed down the half-chewed food with coffee. He looked at Parent, "Decaf?" He did not need caffeine.

"Yes, Holy Grounds sells their blend."

Krachy's eyes focused. He jabbed a last wipe at them with a tissue.

"How did you know about my meeting with Lan at Holy Grounds?" He worked on the croissan'wich which tasted good.

"A member of the Freak Fam is loyal to me as well as to the Freak Fam. I would be a poor leader if I didn't have reach into their group, don't you agree?"

"I do," Krachy covered a burp with his hand, drank more coffee, took another bite. "You should be having this conversation with Jennifer. You realize I'm not the person you need to be worried about, right?"

"Yes," Parent answered, "she's quite dangerous."

Krachy pinned Parent with a steady gaze, his anxiety about the last few minutes ebbing. His look was sullen.

"If you want to stay in business, now's the time to negotiate."

"With her...?"

"Yes, with her, and fast. Just because you say one of your underlings went rouge, doesn't mean that Jennifer won't blame you. For her, this is going to be about what you put in motion." His hand shook as he set the mug down on the table. "You'll be lucky if she doesn't kill you for Sami's kidnapping. Whether you kidnapped her or not may not matter. Also, if I were to guess, she probably knows that I was targeted for assassination earlier. She's good at anticipating next moves. I've learned that from watching her over the past several years."

"But the attempt failed," Parent countered, giving Krachy the eyes you gave someone when you were telling them you were afraid of what could happen next. "I had nothing to do with the man that tried to kill you."

Krachy took a drink. "It won't matter. You need to admit that to yourself and start thinking about damage control, Parent. Start thinking about what you can offer Jennifer so that she'll back down. I'm telling you, she's coming here and her rampage will not be pretty."

"I can offer her my disobedient child, the child that went rouge. But I need your help to get her."

"You act like I know where she is. I don't."

"The woman you call Stone-Face-Lady was one of my Uppers. She and another man set up their own unauthorized operation to terrorize Amanda and Richard." He glanced at the married couple near the hatch then back at Krachy.

"Bald Man is working with the Upper, Stone-Face-Lady, right?" Krachy finished the croissan'wich, taking a last drink of coffee starting to feel better. At least his hands stopped shaking.

"Yes, Maddy, the disobedient Upper you call Stone-Face-Lady, rebelled. The Lower, Bald Man, real name Parkton, is oath sworn to me but that also means he follows the orders of his Upper. Maddy knows this and used Parkton to help her. Parkton doesn't even know Maddy rebelled. He's just following orders. Very little about the extent of any operation the VG undertakes is revealed to Lowers. When Maddy saw that I had changed my mind about taking over Biltmire Station with enhanced people she decided to do it herself. She's very ambitious."

"You make it sound like I should be sympathetic to your cause just because you stopped your takeover plans."

Parent leaned forward on his elbows.

"My takeover was only going to be necessary when Jennifer was arrested and you quit your job."

Krachy's eyes rounded, not buying it.

"But I just decided to leave my job after the riot, after Jennifer was arrested. That's only been a few days. You're telling me that your plan was hatched then canceled that fast?"

Parent leaned back.

"Yes, that's what I'm telling you…" One corner of his mouth arched up.

Krachy looked down at the table considering that, then his head lifted, seeing, but not believing it.

"You're afraid, just like I am, that another group will swoop in and fill the void when the VG is put out of business."

"That's not quite right, Ser Bantor. I'm afraid that Maddy will use her new enhanced weapons to take over the station. I know what kind of person she is, what she's capable of. This started out as a profit grab by me to sell enhanced people on the open market. Now it's a fight for survival with everyone on-station at risk."

"Then Jennifer was right. You were going to sell the categorized people for profit. That was your original intent."

"It was, but when Maddy incited the riot, I changed my mind."

"Maddy started the riot?"

"Yes, she did. She incited the riot for two reasons. One, to get you to leave your position as director of the space station, and two, to frame Jennifer so she would not interfere with her plans. Maddy's going to attempt a hostile takeover of the station, starting with detention. Things are happening fast. Maddy would not have gone this far unless she had in her possession the tools to enhance prisoners. If she can gain numbers fast, she may be unstoppable."

"I didn't steal all of the accelerated computer tissues when I raided your fencing operation, did I?"

"No, I can only believe that Maddy made a deal to supply herself with more ACTs. She's resourceful and calculating."

Krachy had to know.

"The ACTs aren't the only thing needed to enhance people. That small computer device is only good for sending nerve impulses. That thing alone can't be the source of the tremendous power Amanda and Richard have. It just can't be!"

Amanda pulled out a chair and sat down with a smile that split her face, as if she took pride in Parent and all he did to alter her body.

"My legs have been given cybernetic replacement nano-machines. The only way my tissues can stand up to the rigors of using the nano-machines is to implant accelerated computer tissues in each leg that control the pain of using them. The ACTs act like a haptic device. The haptics provide electrical nerve feedback to my brain that say I am not in pain. The haptics also allow my brain to receive sensations of touch and feeling in my legs."

Krachy needed more.

"You need immunosuppressant drugs so that your body will not reject the nano-machines. You have pain. You have a lot of pain."

"The nano-machines that were implanted aren't painful. Actually, the implants heal themselves at a highly accelerated rate. The ACTs are what's painful. The ACTs trick my brain into believing there is no pain when I push the nano-implants past what my old legs could have ever achieved. My brain has to be lied to because it knows my old legs could never stand up to extraordinary strength without pain. I need rejection drugs so my body will not reject the ACTs. The ACTs are liars that my natural physiology want to reject. My body wants to reject the foreign invader that is deceiving my brain. Richard and I must have rejection drugs so we don't go mad from the war of deceit being fought inside our bodies. Even though using the nano-machines is not painful, my brain has to be tricked to believe it. The accelerated computer tissues deceive my brain."

Krachy looked at Parent.

"And you think Maddy has more of the nano-machine implants?"

Parent nodded.

"They're very small. What's worse, or better, depending your point of view, is that the NMs self-replicate. Maddy stole a small sample from me but that was more than enough."

"When I raided your fencing operation I lifted a small box of the ACTs. The container had a thousand of them inside." Krachy was trying to understand.

Amanda explained, "I have ACTs implanted in my legs that control the femoral, fibular, and tibial nerves, plus many others. Maddy was torturing us so that we would break our oath to Parent and conform to her. You rescued us just in time. Thank you!" Amanda's gratitude was genuine it seemed. Her look softened with relief.

"You said that the serial killings were committed by test subjects that failed." Krachy turned to Parent. "You still have a lot to explain."

"—No, you don't understand!" Parent insisted. "The people that committed the murders were failed test subjects of Maddy's. I already admitted I've waited too long to contact you. Maddy has been rouge for over a month."

Krachy was surprised to feel the room shift under his feet. He was no longer on the station. He was on a ship! He'd been so scatter-brained since he sat down he hadn't even considered he could be on a starship. Not to mention the unbelievable journey here was cloudy, to say the least.

Parent saw Krachy's apprehension and grabbed the table as the ship began to pick up speed.

"I find it convenient to keep my interests mobile." He touched a finger to an ear bud, listening, then continued, "It seems I'll get an opportunity to explain everything to Jennifer after all."

This twist did *not* surprise Krachy.

"Jennifer's hailing your ship now, isn't she?"

Parent pulled his finger from his ear and nodded. "Yes."

Krachy knew not to underestimate this man and his knowledge of events. He was quite intelligent. Parent had taken off knowing about this inevitable twist; however, Krachy was resolute.

"I'm not going to bail you out of this, if that's what you're thinking, Parent. I'd be stupid to get in-between Jennifer and her target." Despite himself, Krachy swallowed at the picture of Jennifer unleashing a rage-induced fury on anyone dumb enough to stand between her and a friend in distress, namely Sami.

"I would be foolish to add to Jennifer's wrath. I intercepted a tight beam vid trans Maddy sent to Jennifer from detention…"

"Maddy contacted Jennifer from detention?"

"She did, and that was a mistake. I have contacts inside detention too." One eyebrow rose then fell.

"If Maddy contacted Jennifer, Jennifer probably thinks Maddy's op is being shut down. That's what I would think. Jennifer would also assume that I'd be a target for assassination. But that's not what you're saying, is it…?"

"Well, partly it is. You were a target, but you took care of that yourself. Amanda and Richard were a few minutes late warning you. However, there is one thing Maddy is not so good at—multitasking. While she was pre-occupied trying to have you killed, she forgot to cover her backdoor." Parent smiled for the first time. He had a fatherly smile, not cocky or all knowing, just humble, reasonable.

Krachy was hesitant to think it. It was too good to be true.

Parent nodded, easing Krachy toward it anyway…

"You rescued Sami, didn't you?"

Parent thinned his lips.

"While Amanda and Richard came to warn you about the Stealth-Man assassin, yes I did."

"You knew that might pull you out of Jennifer's line-of-fire."

"All I ask is that you help me talk with Jennifer? Can you do that for me, us?" Parent's eyes gathered in his children. They both came to his side, their hopeful eyes landing on Krachy.

"Is that what you need my help with? You keep asking for my help to stop Maddy, but talking to Jennifer for you won't accomplish that."

A knock came at the hatch. It opened. Sami stood in the hatchway then took in a breath of relief, which gave Krachy a split second to stand before she rushed the short distance hugging his guts out. Krachy pulled back.

"You okay?"

Sami's smile lit up the room.

"Now I am!"

Krachy looked past Sami seeing the stick of a woman that waited just outside the hatch. The woman had hollow cheeks and skin that grabbed at her face over a boney skull. The woman's hair was unremarkable brownish. She adjusted the bandage over her nose like she was clearing her airway. Her voice was nasal.

"Krachy," she didn't look all that pleased to see Krachy, but the corner of her mouth ticked.

Krachy pushed back from Sami taking a step toward the woman.

"Nace."

Nace Notchins extended a hand, but before she knew what was going on, Krachy swung his arms around the taller woman pulling her close. He pushed back and looked up into her eyes.

"Thank you." Krachy released her.

Nace still wasn't used to the nasal dilator strip across her broken nose and started to pull a hand up to adjust it before she spoke.

Krachy caught her wrist and pulled Nace's open palm to his mouth kissing it.

"No, I mean it," he insisted as she tried to shed his grip. "Thank you for getting her out. Sami's like a niece to me."

The aftermath of Jennifer's handiwork was all too evident on Nace's face. Her eyes were blood shot and both under eyes were black. Nace's nasal trill was loud with each breath.

"I'm not the noble warrior your future wifey is, Bantor." She tried to snort, but it turned into a throat-clearing hack. "I'm getting paid."

"So?"

The hard look on Nace's face mellowed.

"You didn't have to help, at any price. God bless you, woman!"

His smile pulled Nace's hate for Krachy's alter-ego future wifey down a notch—not a notch, a "notchins."

"She's still a bitch!" Nace squawked, referring to Jennifer.

Krachy shrugged.

"Sometimes, yeah, I can see that."

Krachy turned to Parent, at the same time grabbing Sami's hand to feel her warmth.

"I told you I'm not going to bail you out of this, Parent." He glanced at Sami briefly, "Even though I'm thankful you saved Sami."

Parent held up a hand.

"—I don't need you to go commando and storm detention, Ser Bantor. You have other skills that can help put an end to this mess. I'm asking you to use those skills to help, that's all."

Krachy squeezed Sami's hand before releasing it. His temper was rising because Parent was talking in circles and this was not the time to be doing that.

Nace turned to leave. By reflex Krachy snatched her arm.

"Hey, where are you going?" Nace tried to pull free, but Krachy stepped around her blocking the exit.

Nace's breath picked up. Her nasal trill echoed in the small room.

"I got paid and I'm outta here. Move!"

"You know Maddy intends to use prisoners as test subjects and implant things into their bodies to make them follow her orders. A long time ago, you and I took an oath when we where at the training academy together. We took an oath to protect. We were young, but I still remember. I know you do too. You bunked right across the hall from me at the academy. We helped each other get through that eight weeks of hell."

"Move!" Nace tried to skirt past him.

Krachy pushed at her arms.

"C'mon, Nace, you and me go back a long way. Don't do this. Huh? You can honor that oath. We can team up again. What'd ya say?"

The trill got wet with snot. Nace swallowed to clear her throat.

"I'd smack you if my face wasn't wasted from that girl-friend of yours! You're trying to play me just like your woman did. She set me up like she was used to setting people up. You're both manipulative bastards. I got my creds and I'm done with all this shit!"

"All right," Krachy stood aside. "You go, that's your choice. But know this, Nace. I need your help. I'm not asking for Jennifer. I'm asking for me. *I* need your help. Please."

Nace swung around glaring at Parent.

"You didn't tell me Krachy was gonna be here! You're a manipulative bastard too!" A bubble of snot shot out a nostril. Nace threw a frustrated sleeve at the mess and rubbed too hard by accident. "Shit that hurt!"

Parent looked at Krachy, and said deadpan, "This is what I needed your help with, Ser Bantor."

Krachy was flabbergasted. Nace was right. Parent *was* a manipulative bastard! Parent knew all along his plant inside detention, Nace, was going to refuse to take the next step to bring Maddy down *unless* Krachy was around to convince her otherwise.

Krachy tried to get past his anger about being played.

"Nace, you pulled Sami out of there. You still have the moves! Rescuing Sami couldn't have been easy, especially in your condition."

Nace thinned her lips.

"I walked right out the intake hatch with her. I'm takin' the easy creds. I'm done I said!" But she didn't storm off, didn't flinch to leave. She was warming to the cause. Nace wanted a purpose. She was just too pissed off at everyone and everything all of the time to admit it.

"Let me ask you this," Krachy said. "You're on the inside. Who else does Maddy have helping her? She can't be doing this alone."

"The nurse for one."

"Figures. Maddy would need medical help to perform implant surgery on prisoners."

"That was how I grabbed Sami and left. Maddy and the nurse were alone with a prisoner. I saw my chance and I took it."

"You still have the moves." Krachy gave her the once-over.

"Piss off! That's not going to work. I'm already banged up enough. I'm not gonna lead an armed assault on detention just 'cause you want to save your job, or whatever."

"Nace, you know that's not how I roll. I've never been a glory hound. You know I haven't."

"Yeah, I know. But you're a damn good liar."

"Unavoidable in my job, but I don't lie to friends, never have."

"What are you saying?"

"When we finish with Maddy, like I know you and I are gonna do, you run detention when it's over. You run it the right way, to make sure this never happens again. You make sure the prisoners get the treatment they deserve. There is always room at the top. Don't let them tell you there is not!"

Nace took a turn at being flabbergasted. Her trilling slowed to a steady, low whistle.

"What'd ya say?" Krachy pulled her palm to his mouth and planted a loud smooch on it.

Nace jerked her hand away. "Stop that! And stop trying to bribe me."

Krachy's eyes rounded. "I thought that was important to you."

If Krachy didn't know her so well, he wouldn't have caught the hard right jab meant for his chin. He let go of her wrist. His eyes twinkled.

Nace swallowed to clear mucus, her brows snapped together.

"I'm gonna kiss you on the mouth. It'll hurt." Krachy's lashes fluttered.

Nace looked surprised, but her eyes didn't give an inch.

"Tongue or not?" Krachy closed in.

Nace shot out a hand pushing his face away.

"I said stop that! You always were a persistent little bugger."

"That's not my best trait," he grinned.

"I said enough already! Besides, you're damaged goods. You always did like tall women." Nace was tired, from her injuries or the internal struggle to do the right thing, it wasn't clear. She took a seat and blew out a soggy trill.

A croissan'wich and coffee was placed on the table in front of Nace. Krachy caught a glimpse of the person that placed the food on the table then left promptly through the hatch. Parent sat quietly, folded his hands on the table, and looked at Sami. Sami sat down next to him and eyed the food. She looked tired too.

Nace pushed the croissan'wich at Sami.

"I sound like a bulldog lappin' water when I eat. You take it."

Sami grabbed the warm croissan'wich and took a few bites.

"Thanks, and not just for this," her eyes glistened.

Nace dipped her head at the coffee. Sami took a drink.

"All right, I guess I could use a pay raise." Nace looked at Krachy as he took the last chair at the table.

Krachy winked.

"I said all right! Enough with that, Krachy!"

"Okay, I'll ease up. But this is your show too, Nace. You tell us how we can re-take detention."

Nace sniffed. "I'd take a page from your space-tart's playbook."

Krachy smiled.

"Yeah, can you say HUNGER STRIKE?" Nace's grin was evil.

FIFTEEN

Krachy watched Jennifer exit the shuttle that had just touched down in the landing bay on Parent's ship. He was surprised to see a look of calm resolve planted on her face. She did not look pissed off. Jennifer stopped a few feet away from the greeting party looking at each person until she settled on Sami, the one person she loved like a niece.

"Can you give me a hug? I need it."

Sami brushed past Parent and swung her arms around Jennifer in a jarring grasp. After a few moments Sami tried to release her, but Jennifer would not let go.

"Hey, I'm okay," Sami whispered into Jennifer's ear, "really." Jennifer released her, and Sami turned to look at Nace standing behind Parent next to Krachy.

Nace turned to leave through the landing bay hatch, but Krachy snagged her wrist. Nace made a half-hearted attempt to break free, then turned as Jennifer stepped over to face her. Nace dipped her head so she didn't have to look Jennifer in the eyes.

"I apologize," Jennifer said bending at the knees to try to look up into Nace's downturned face. "When you dropped your guard I attacked you. It wasn't a fair fight." She raised her palms showing Nace she regretted what she'd done.

"Your man tried to stick his tongue down my throat." Nace looked at Jennifer trying to get a rise out of her any way she could. It was lame and childish, but it was a way to vent nonetheless.

Jennifer didn't answer, and finally Nace sighed.

"I accept your apology, I guess. Besides, I got in a gut shot on you," Nace's frown turned up slightly, but with no great enthusiasm. "Your man is a sneaky little turd. He plays the angles, pushes all the right buttons. I can't believe I agreed to help him."

Jennifer moved so close Nace had no choice but to look in her eyes.

"What?"

"I'm very sincere when I tell you how much it means to me to have Sami back. No words, I have no words to express my gratitude. We're okay, you and me, right?"

Nace seemed even more uncomfortable, but raised a corner of her mouth.

"Forget it," she hated giving in but the situation she'd fallen into was bigger than her anger it seemed.

"You can bail out of this if you want." Jennifer took a step back.

Nace looked surprised, then glanced away as if the weight of Jennifer's offer was insulting. The offer to run and do nothing must have been just the right incentive to awake Nace's determination because she took in a loud, wet breath, inflating her chest.

"I'm no coward, Bane. Don't play that card with me! I can stand toe-to-toe with the best of 'em!" Nace took a step toward Jennifer getting all up in her face. "Next time give me a little warning, and I'll prove it to you!"

Jennifer backed away, her hands up.

"I have no doubt. Let's not go there. I don't want another thunder-thump to my stomach. Besides, if my head takes any more damage I could end up mumbling my way to old age. I submit." She extended a hand, glancing down at it, then back into Nace's eyes.

Krachy sidled up next to Nace, nudging her elbow with an arm. Nace shot a pissed off look at him.

"Don't crowd me, shorty! I'm still debating if I wanna work with your hellion here."

Jennifer added, "Thank you for Sami."

Nace's muscles relaxed, the wet exhale proof she could do good and like it. She grabbed Jennifer's hand shaking it.

Jennifer let go and shot a relieved look at Krachy that said, *Yes, I'm glad you're alive too.* Krachy smiled at her.

Jennifer swiveled her head as she looked at the shuttle, alert and excited.

Nace followed Jennifer's eyes landing on a stocky dark-haired man that jumped down onto the deck from the shuttle.

Sami saw Dimitri Volodya and ran to meet him throwing her arms around his neck and pulling his mouth against hers in a passionate kiss. They released and spoke lowly to each other glancing at Nace a few times as they did.

Nace's face twisted as Sami and Dimirti held hands striding right up to her.

Nace tried to step back but Jennifer and Krachy blocked her retreat with their bodies.

Nace's expression hardened, but before she could tell Jennifer and Krachy to leave her alone, Dimitri went down on one knee and looked up at her.

"This is for you and us." He then turned to look up into Sami's eyes. Sami's face turned scarlet.

"I've been waiting for this moment for all of my life. I'm going to take all the love that I have in my heart, and let it all out. Sami, I'm going to make you feel the impact of my soul!" Dimitri swallowed. "Marry me."

Sami gasped. Her eyes welled up with tears. She looked at Nace.

"This is what doing good looks like, Nace." She turned back to Dimitri, nodding hard, "Yes, yes, oh, yes I will!"

Dimitri stood and the two of them hugged and laughed rocking back and forth. Dimitri looked past Sami into Nace's eyes, extending an arm to pull Nace toward them. Nace half-scowled, and tried to resist, but Krachy and Jennifer pushed her toward the happy couple.

Jennifer whispered in Nace's ear, "Go ahead, get some."

Nace reached unconsciously at her nose bandage but before she could adjust it, Krachy pushed her hand at Dimitri's back, then crowded her back-side with his body forcing her to join in on the team hug.

Nace still resisted.

"Here, let me show you," Krachy then opened both arms pulling Nace into Dimitri and Sami locking his arms around all three of them. Nace's rigid, defiant body began to bleed the anger she carried like a slow puncture leaking air. The release came out her nostrils in steady, grated snorts. Sami eyed her and laughed. Nace's eyes shot open embarrassed. Then Nace finally smiled too, not fighting her bull-dog-snorkel-sounds any longer.

Krachy pulled back. By then Nace was jerking her head up-and-down, smiling hard, and snorting away with abandon. Dimitri laughed at her snorts as all three of them hugged and laughed.

Jennifer turned to the man she didn't know.

Krachy watched Jennifer take in Parent with her eyes. He gulped realizing that no matter what, Jennifer's volcanic temper could erupt at any minute framed in the context that Parent had started this whole disaster in motion. He was floored when Jennifer smiled at him.

"I'm changing my ways. I don't want revenge on you, whoever you are."

"I'm the person that started all this but who now wants it to end the right way." Parent looked in her eyes accepting Jennifer's judgment.

Krachy studied Jennifer and was surprised to see her retreat from her old self. Her inner-self could not order her outer self, her outer injured self, to extract payment for what

Parent was responsible for. Jennifer was nothing short of a different person. Krachy was watching her transform right in front of his eyes. The most impressive part of her metamorphosis was that there seemed to be no struggle pushing Jennifer toward this new normal. Krachy had been wrong about her, so wrong that he felt ashamed. Krachy had told Parent that Jennifer was a killer, a person that would loose an anger-fueled rampage when she landed.

"I'm the head of the VG. One of my children has gone rouge and is responsible for what's happened."

"I've caused a lot of trouble too."

"Yes, you have, Ms. Bane. Here," Parent motioned for Jennifer and Krachy to move away from the laugh-pack so they could talk privately. "Let's move so your friends can bond."

Jennifer and Krachy followed Parent toward the landing bay blast hatch and stopped.

"My name is Parent. Maddy is not shutting down her operation. She's just ramping up." Parent scowled like he was wondering what he had done to be jinxed with a child that was ruining his life.

Jennifer glanced at the laugh-pack as if trying to pull positive vibes from them then wet her lips.

"I believe you when you say Maddy is responsible for all this." She jabbed a look at Krachy who nodded.

"Maddy is trying to gain numbers, enhanced numbers, to make a play to take over the whole station," Parent explained.

Jennifer shook her head. "Won't happen."

"But if she has inroads into detention she must have inroads into Station Security too. Her deceit and resourcefulness can't be underestimated. It seems to me that Sami's escape was far too easy. Maddy may have let Sami escape with Nace. I wouldn't put anything past her."

"I believe I had something to do with that."

Parent frowned looking down, then his head lifted.

Jennifer darkened.

"I made it a point to let Maddy know everything she thought about me was true."

"The tight beam vid trans…"

"Yes, the tight beam vid trans."

"You cut the feed before Maddy could deliver her demands."

"You'll never know how hard that was, Parent. But it seemed to have worked." Jennifer glanced at the laugh-pack that had untangled and were talking casually now.

Parent thought he understood.

"You made Maddy think no matter what she did, you'd still come for her."

"That's at least *one* of the reasons Sami is standing over there with her new fiancé, Parent. You and Nace are the other. Thank you." Jennifer's look softened.

Parent smiled, "You're welcome," then, "But Maddy is right, I can tell…" His brows lifted the grin evaporating.

"Doesn't matter who is part of Maddy's team in detention or in Sta Sec," Jennifer said coldly. "I'm going to end this *my* way. You in?"

"I have to be in! You've shut down most of my business. I like being in business, my children like being in business. They'll be no business left if you keep on the way you're going. The sooner we end this the better. Besides, Nace has a good idea how to flush Maddy out of detention."

Jennifer ignored his last statement.

"You started all this. But I said I don't want revenge."

"What do you want?"

"I want you to do the right thing. A lot of people have been affected by this, not just me."

Parent nodded quietly. "I'm listening."

"You're going to have some new children to take care of."

Parent's eyes narrowed readying himself for the punch line.

"First off, I've rescued a bunch of people off of a space lab that were tissue donors for Maddy's enhancement operation." Jennifer paused, a look of disgust on her face. "I want these people cared for. I want them to have a chance at a good life, a meaningful life. They should be treated with dignity and given a purpose. You understand what I'm saying?"

"I think so," Parent responded numbly, calculating the math in his head with no real joy.

"I want the people I rescued that are capable of working to be given jobs. I'd like the ones that are not capable of working to be taken care of. I want them to receive medical treatment and ongoing care so they can live out what's left of their life with propriety."

"You want a lot, Ms. Bane."

Jennifer held up a hand, "That's not all I want. There are a lot of people on Biltmire Station that have lost loved ones, family members. These people are going to need something from you as well."

The scale Jennifer was proposing pulled some color from Parent's face. Given that Parent was a black man, it was stark.

"Yes, the families that lost people to whom they thought was a serial killer will need help getting past that tragedy. People also lost family in the riot. I want you to set up an aid organization, kind of like a post-trauma assistance center. I want this assistance center to be funded by the VG, then all the donations that come in once it gets started reinvested in the center. The center can help with job placement for the tissue-donor people I rescued off Cimmerian Space Lab. The center can set up an assisted living and skilled nursing facility for the tissue-donor people that are not able to work. And this center can offer grief counseling and therapy for anyone that qualifies due to the mock serial killings and riot that took place on-station."

"The VG does charity work, but this is way beyond that."

Jennifer turned down the corners of her mouth staring icily into Parent's eyes.

"This is NOT a negotiation!"

Dimitri, ever vigilant to the needs of his liege lord, heard the inflection in Jennifer's voice. He jerked his head at Jennifer then sprinted to her side leaving Sami and Nace where they were.

Jennifer looked at him briefly.

"Dimitri is my sworn vassal. Either he or I, or both of us, will supervise the creation of your new not-for-profit center. Any questions?"

Parent's mouth fell open. At the same time Nace and Sami stepped up beside Jennifer.

Sami chimed in. "I'll help too."

Nace eyed Parent and shrugged. "Count me in. What are we doing?"

Jennifer smiled smugly. Parent was outnumbered it seemed. Even though he was on his own ship and could get all the backup he needed, he thought better of it. There was no mistaking the fact that Jennifer was not alone. And it was not just the people standing beside her. Parent knew Jennifer had three starships at her disposal. Jennifer could back up her demands. She'd proved that by running her destructive blockage over the last few days. Parent came to the realization that if he wanted to stay in business, yielding to Jennifer was going to be a cost he could not avoid.

Jennifer looked at Krachy. "Can we talk?"

Parent watched Jennifer and Krachy step away to chat and for the first time felt Nace was right about Jennifer. Jennifer could be a real bitch. The amiable, fatherly demeanor Parent wore like a shield was developing deep gashes of doubt. Parent doubted that he'd be able to control how any of this mess ended. It was sobering, but inevitable. He'd made bad mistakes indeed.

"Did someone try to kill you, love?" Jennifer asked as soon as they were out of ear-shot.

Krachy didn't say anything for several seconds. Finally he answered.

"Yes."

When Jennifer's breath caught, Krachy added, "Same stealth-guy that tried to kill you." He chuckled nervously in attempt to calm Jennifer down, trying to act like it was no big deal. "He won't be sneaking up on anyone else again."

"I'm so sorr—" Jennifer tried to say, accepting blame. Krachy shot his hand to her mouth briefly.

"Shhh," he breathed. "What'd you find out?" Krachy tried to move past it so Jennifer would.

"Bald Man was heading back to Cimmerian Space Lab to pick up more tissue donors for this Maddy person. We captured him and shut down Maddy's pipeline of raw human materials for good."

"Did you know that Sami was being held in Biltmire Detention?"

"Yes, when we shut down the space lab that was supplying Maddy, I rescued a bunch of unfortunate people that were the source of the raw materials. One of the women lost her eyes so she used her enhanced hearing to help us pinpoint Sami's location."

"Are you going to give Parent back the booty we took?"

"I thought about jettisoning all of the booty on my way back here, but decided against it."

"Leverage?"

"Yeah, I figured I might need it as a bargaining chip for, for, whatever." She extended a hand rubbing Krachy's cheek. "If you were in trouble, I would have traded it for you. God, I'm glad I didn't have to do that!" Jennifer smiled.

Krachy grabbed her hand and pushed her palm to his lips kissing it. Startled, Jennifer felt Nace ease up beside her and turned.

"Your turn, get some." Nace canted her head at Krachy.

Jennifer smiled at her then turned to Krachy planting an open mouth kiss on his lips.

Nace retreated, returned to the others.

Jennifer came out of the kiss from Krachy with apprehension wrinkling her forehead.

"You're still going to marry me aren't you?"

Krachy realized Jennifer had been putting on a show for Parent. She was scared how all this muck was going to affect their relationship even though she'd never precipitated any of it. Jennifer had to stay strong in front of Parent to get what she wanted, but her bravado was synth pap thin. She tried to shoulder too much of the load to a fault.

Krachy would have none of it and quickly responded.

"Only if the ceremony is a double."

Jennifer glanced down not understanding, then looked over at Dimitri and Sami and turned back to Krachy.

"That's the best idea I've ever heard in my life!"

"Four person honeymoon too then?" Krachy grinned crookedly.

Jennifer bobbed her head up-and-down smiling.

"Nace wants to cut off Maddy's food supply to flush her out of detention."

Jennifer exhaled shaking her head.

"Not needed."

Krachy squinted.

"I know how Maddy is going to try to take over the entire space station."

"With numbers, with more enhanced prisoners to get a force behind her, right?"

"No, love. That would take too long. Too many things could go wrong. Also, Maddy knows we could just cut off her food to smoke her out of her rat hole in detention. What Maddy is planning is much more simple than that. Trust me."

"How do you know that, Jennifer?"

Jennifer straightened and gave him her most confident smile.

"Marco taught me well. You haven't seen the people I rescued off the raw material space lab. The answer was written all over what's *left* of the faces on the poor people Maddy had carved up."

"I don't understand."

"You will when you see the rescued people and I explain it to you. Maddy has already moved on, left detention, and is planning her next set of moves. She let Nace take Sami out of detention because she needed more time. This little reunion right now was planned by Maddy, Krachy. This women is very smart, very devious."

Krachy considered that and thought back to what Parent said about Maddy.

"Parent said that Maddy's resourcefulness should not be underestimated. How do you know Maddy is so calculating?"

"I've been forced to deal with people like her before. Nothing Maddy can plan will surpass my understanding of how people like her think. I have too much experience to fall for any diversion like 'starting with detention.' Maddy has tools available to her that I have not seen before. Even though the tools are not the same flavor of tools I've seen before, their use is definitely predictable."

"You think this reunion right now was planned by Maddy?"

"Without a doubt! This reunion has given Maddy time to take what she needs from detention. The items Maddy needed from detention were people. Specific people matching a very specific physical description. Maddy has already moved on to her next target. There's no question of it. The only question is, have I thought enough steps ahead of her?"

"And you think you've thought far enough ahead to stop her?"

Jennifer pushed her tongue under her upper lip, her lips thinning.

"I think I can stop her with my next move or the move after that. Regardless, what I have planned next will inject real doubt in Maddy's mind that she can pull off her takeover. I ran my plan by Marco a half hour ago. He just grinned and nodded his head. What does that tell you?"

"Pay dirt! Right?"

"Right."

"Speaking of pay," Parent had come to a halt next to Jennifer and Krachy. "Can you please return the items you liberated from me on-station and in space during the blockade?"

Jennifer looked at Krachy letting him handle it.

"After we stop Maddy, you'll get everything we grabbed on-station and in space except for the accelerated computer tissues," Krachy assured him.

Jennifer spoke up.

"I captured a number of people in space that are a part of the VG or would have been a part of the VG if they had made it onto Biltmire. I also confiscated quite a bit of booty that was going to be delivered to several of your on-station businesses."

Parent's forehead crinkled.

"Yes, your blockade. You hit me hard on and off-station. Let me ask you this—From your demands about universal care for the people from that space lab, I assume the children you captured of mine are being treated well. Yes?"

"Of course."

"I was expecting a number of women to arrive on-station that are providers at the adult men's clubs I run. They never showed up. There were also some hard-working ethnic ladies that work in the massage parlors I run. They haven't arrived either. There were at least two *whales* that jumped in via starship from out-system that never checked-in to enjoy all the comps I intended to give them for gambling, and losing, at my casino. These two whales are extremely rich gamblers who bet extraordinarily large amounts of creds. I went to a great deal of trouble to lavishly out-comp a pleasure base that was trying to get these two high rollers to gamble at their establishment instead of mine. Women like these two whales can make or break my casino's take this financial quarter. You, Miss Bane, have hit my bottom line very hard by snagging them out of space and taking them prisoner as part of your blockage."

"Hey, give me a break! I was just hitting anything and everything during the blockade. I had no other choice. You and I are talking, figuring this out, aren't we? I intend to instruct my team to ease-up, stand down, whatever."

Parent let out a breath. He had to get past the fact that his businesses had almost come to a complete halt because of Jennifer. Parent decided to be indulgent focusing on what he learned from all this instead. He looked at Krachy.

"You exposed quite a weakness in my on-station security sneaking into my fencing and gleam operations through the O^2 air ducts inside each room." He shook his head.

"No ill effects from the diethyl ether gas I used on your children then?" Krachy asked referring to the people he gassed so he could snag the booty from both places.

"One of my children was nauseous and threw up, but otherwise, no."

"I apologize for that. I didn't mean to injure anyone."

"I should have known the Freak Fam could use the O^2 air ducts the way you did. Part of that is my fault."

"You realize I do have reservations about giving back the Gleam inhalers, right, Parent? Drugs are drugs. I don't want to see anyone harmed using them."

Parent's patience with his lack of control over this entire situation began to show. He took in an agitated breath and shuddered slowly letting it out.

"I'll try to even the scale, Ser Bantor. Not everything I participate in is illegal." Parent's voice rose unable to hide his mounting frustration.

"How much of a stake do you have in Food Theory?" Krachy asked.

Jennifer's eyebrows hiked, interested in the answer. She now had a friend that was part of that equation—Carol.

"Ten percent," Parent said after a moment. "At least you don't think that's illegal and needs to be shut down too!" The snip in his retort was sharp. Parent was not used to being questioned about his businesses, let alone having any of them shut down.

Jennifer stayed silent. *What a luxury,* she thought to herself: *Krachy has the same morals I do.* Jennifer thought about what Lan had said to Krachy when teamwork took the forefront: *Don't get misty on me!* Well, Jennifer was swimming in a misty cloud of love for Krachy. He was everything in a man she had ever wanted. Narrow ass and all.

Parent's head swiveled toward Jennifer.

"Why are you smiling?" Parent took in gulps of air thinking that Jennifer liked seeing him lose his cool in front of her.

"I didn't say a thing," Jennifer's smile lingered. "Krachy's still going to marry me. I'm totally fine, Parent."

"Can I say without offending you, that you can be a real bitch, Ms. Bane? You like seeing me sweat, lose my temper." Parent looked at Krachy, "You too, Ser Bantor. Remember, I had Amanda and Richard come to warn you earlier? I was trying to do the right thing!"

"With all the speed they possess, they were too late."

"No respec—!" Parent snapped his mouth shut.

"Hey," Krachy held up both hands. "Calm down, okay? I had to kill a man to save myself. I'm the one that should be pissed off!"

Jennifer looked concerned but calm. Her man was alive. That's all that mattered. However, there was still more to be done.

"You've seen the type of people you've been up against, Parent—my team. I suggest you calm down and not make me regret foregoing any revenge on you."

Her eyes narrowed piercing Parent's skin like a laser. Jennifer would be damned if she was going to let this man disrespect Krachy.

"I'm the one you have ask permission from to stay in business. Just roll with that and get used to it. Understand?" The finality of the question was no question at all.

It was hard to tell, but Parent's face seemed to redden. He was furious about his inability to control this situation. Instead of exploding like he wanted to, Parent figured he'd better move things along so he could finish this catastrophe. He was going to have to figure out a way to fund all the crap he was now on the hook for, and to figure out a way to make up for all the lost revenue Jennifer's damn blockade pulled from his pocket.

"You know if we're going to be working together you should start treating me like a partner, not a pariah," Parent said sharply.

"Fair enough—There is just one thing before I ask you to turn your ship around and dock on Biltmire Station. You're going to have to change the name of the VG. *Violence Group* is not going to cut it any longer."

"What? That name comes from a long past group of easterners on earth, the Yakuza. It doesn't mean anything, just tradition."

"Too bad, you're going to have to turn it around. How about GV: *Good Vibes* instead?"

Parent huffed.

"Fine! Whatever!" He looked past Jennifer at the shuttle desperate to move things along. "Who else did you bring with you?"

"My support team, six people in all. They're going to help us end this."

Parent nodded reluctantly, then spoke lowly into the sub vocal mic on his throat. Within seconds the large battle ship began to change course.

SIXTEEN

"I hope you can make more sense of what I found out than I can." Nace Notchins approached Jennifer once she returned to the landing bay where Parent's ship was docked on Biltmire Space Station. Nace had just completed a recon visit to Biltmire Detention.

"Try me." Jennifer glanced at the hand comp in Nace's hand, then back at her face.

"The detention nurse, she's gone, outta there. The nurse didn't leave any word why, she just left detention and has not been seen since. My captain had to request a replacement for her, and already had the second shift RN come to work to fill in. I figure Maddy needs someone with medical skills."

"You're right, Maddy needs medical help with her enhancement operations. What else?"

Nace turned the small screen toward Jennifer briefly, then pulled it back studying it.

"I can synch this so your tea—"

Jennifer stopped Nace with a raised hand, "—Our, *our* team, Nace." Jennifer thinned her lips.

Nace blinked a few times trying on the teamwork vibe to see how it fit.

"Yeah, okay, our team. I can synch the data to our team for analysis, but I can tell you right now several prisoners have been taken from detention. A sergeant that works with Maddy walked the prisoners right out the exit hatch. Detention control let them leave. Prisoner transfers are common so it all looked normal. I have the list, here."

"I guessed as much. Descriptions?"

"What?"

"What are the physical descriptions of the prisoners that were taken, Nace?"

"What does that have to do with anything?"

"What the prisoners look like has everything to do with what Maddy is planning."

Nace reached unconsciously at her nose bandage then rubbed the side of her head.

"You know my head still hurts," she said, still unable to get past Jennifer's whip-ass in Carol's cell a few days ago. Annoyed was a hard thing to shed for Nace; that's just the way she was.

Jennifer was patient. She knew how annoyed Nace was in general. In fact, Jennifer had used that against Nace in Carol's cell as part of her escape plan. However, Jennifer was not going to remind Nace about that. Now was the time move on and march forward. Jennifer waited.

"You don't take the bait very easy do you, Bane?"

"Please, just Jennifer. Okay?"

"I asked you a question…Jennifer."

"I can't afford to."

"Why's that?"

"Too many people count on me. A lot of people are counting on you too."

"Me?"

"The information you retrieved is the key to whether my theory about what Maddy is planning next is right or not. If the descriptions of the prisoners match my theory, I can stop her. If not, I may not have a way to stop her. We were counting on you to get that data and you did. It's the key to everything at this point."

Nace scrutinized Jennifer trying to decide if she believed her or not. She did.

Murphy strode up to the two women.

"I have my synch mate turned on. Can you send me the data now, Nace? It's too valuable to be on just one hand comp."

Nace stared at her.

"Nace?" Murphy prodded.

Nace cleared her throat.

"Yeah, sure," she fingered the screen then an audible chirp confirmed the data was now on at least two HCs.

Murphy glanced down at her hand comp, then back at Nace.

"Thank you. Can you come with me so I can get your take on what you remember about the prisoners that were taken? You're the only person that may have seen or talked to them. Even though the data says one thing you might remember something else." Murphy retreated a step toward Parent's battle ship behind her.

Nace stabbed a look at Jennifer who also turned toward Parent's ship. For an obvious reason this seemed like a big step for Nace. Nace's agreement to be a part of Jennifer's team was a big step, as was being an equally important part of the team. Nace followed Murphy up the cargo ramp into Parent's ship.

Jennifer watched Nace and Murphy disappear into the belly of the battle ship as Carol, Lan, Aretha, and Ian McKivey meandered down the cargo ramp. Aretha held Ian's arm and Jennifer noticed that Ian was resting a hand on Aretha's grip. Aretha was short next to Ian but looked very happy for some reason.

Ian saw the smile on Jennifer's face when he stopped short in front of her. He smiled back.

"Aretha's a fox."

Aretha looked happy then dropped her grip from Ian's arm reaching around his backside for an affectionate grope. Jennifer could see the muscles in Aretha's arm flexing as she massaged Ian's behind.

"Focus people," Lan instructed referring to the two of them. "We still have some work to do."

Aretha stopped what she was doing then lifted her chin toward Ian's face. Ian pulled her close with a long arm around her lower back and locked lips. The air escaping his nostrils was loud as the two of them carried on with no concern for the audience around them.

Jennifer was glad to see Ian happy. All she could think about was, *How nice it is to see some good come from all this muddle.* She crossed her arms taking in the scene.

Lan stepped up beside Jennifer and nudged an elbow into her ribs, not very hard, but attention getting nonetheless. Nace's thunderclap was still tender in Jennifer's chest. She gasped.

"The hell!?" Jennifer grabbed her side. "Whad'ya do that for?"

"You and your Short Man Hunk get sentimental at the wrong times."

Jennifer rubbed at her side, eyes burning into Lan's.

"You could have just said something!"

Carol interrupted, "Jennifer?"

Jennifer turned.

"We're getting ready to risk a lot here. Please focus, okay?"

Jennifer let out a ragged breath.

"All right, but we still have to wait for a few thing—" Jennifer felt the hand comp in her pocket vibrate, she pulled it out and studied the screen. "Good, no more waiting for Murphy, she's done analyzing Nace's recon data. The physical descriptions of the prisoners that were taken from detention by Maddy match my theory. The guy in the apartment we're paying an unexpected visit to matches the description of a prisoner that Maddy took from detention as well. We're a go."

The blast hatch beside Jennifer opened. Channing Altimer held an anti-grav control joystick in his hand. Jennifer backed out of the way so Channing could lead the livestock shipping container into the landing bay. The anti-grav container moved silently through the hatch, then Channing powered down the anti-grav unit bringing the rectangular five-foot high, nine-feet long shipping container to rest. The blast hatch shut behind Channing and he looked at Jennifer.

"I got a used one like you suggested." He crinkled his nose. "It smells inside."

Jennifer didn't really need to be told; the air holes that were spaced uniformly down the sides let the fragrant putrescence waft out in all directions.

"No problem, Channing, I just can't take the risk of being seen before we can end this thing. If Sta Sec spots me on-station I'll get pinched again. I figured a used livestock container would do the trick of hiding me while we make our way to the guy's apartment we're going to kidnap. And the smell would probably prevent anyone from getting too curious about what was inside—namely, me. " Jennifer turned to Carol and Lan. "You two ready to go?"

"Yes," Carol looked at Lan who nodded, then back at Jennifer. "You'll need to give us 15 minutes to set up. The guy's apartment is not that far from here and Lan said she knows a pretty quick route under-deck. I can't keep my hand comp turned on. If it goes off, or a call comes in, the noise may give away our position. In fact, I'm not even taking it with me." Carol's look turned thoughtful. "You good with that?"

Jennifer glanced at her hand comp to check station time. She looked from Lan to Carol. "Yeah, that should work. I'll arrive at his apartment at 4:00am. That's twenty minutes from now. He should still be asleep when I wake him up. When you hear me at his apartment hatch, you two can make your move. But wait for Amanda and Richard to do their thing. I want him to get a very clear picture that I'm not a killer or kidnapper."

Carol twisted a cheek. "Relax, I'm not gonna spoil anything, Lan either. We know this may be your chance to prove your innocence. Chill."

Jennifer's forehead tightened. She was getting tired of Carol big-sistering her every chance she got.

"Touchy, isn't she?" Aretha remarked to Carol.

Jennifer's eyes popped open. "Stop ganging up on me!"

How the heck Aretha knew Jennifer's anger just ticked-up was a complete mystery. The women was blind…but certainly not unaware. In fact, Aretha seemed aware of everything around her to the point that it was almost creepy.

Ian reached for Jennifer.

"You need another hug before we conclude this thing?" He made a move to wrap his arms around her.

Jennifer jabbed a hand into his chest.

"You too, McKivey! I've got enough crap to deal with right now. Don't encourage Carol and Aretha!"

Aretha again, somehow, had the spacial recognition to know exactly where Ian's outstretched arms were. She grabbed Ian's wrist and twisted his palm planting it firmly on her right breast.

Ian accepted the grip and squeezed.

Aretha cooed, "I offer fourth for grabbage my chestal area, oh Ian, My Master."

Jennifer rolled her eyes. "Enough with that! You two have the hots for each other, we get it!"

Aretha let Ian go right on squeezing. "Jealous?" She asked Jennifer. "I can show Krachy how to take advantage of my blossoms pressed together and offered fourth for explicit grabbage, if you think he needs practice." Her brows rose stretching the sutures knitting each eye lid sewn shut.

"You and McKivey are made for each other, jeez!"

Ian let go of the Aretha's firm bosom and smiled.

Jennifer eyes bore into Lan's.

"Aren't you going to say something to Aretha and Ian for getting misty at the wrong time? You dinged me!"

Lan ignored her, looked at Carol, "Let's go." Lan led Carol over to the corner of the landing bay into the maintenance closet and closed the hatch. She and Carol had already found a floor grate that would give them access to under-deck inside the closet.

Jennifer's chest heaved staring at the closed maintenance hatch.

Aretha touched Jennifer's shoulder, pulling. "Hey."

Jennifer turned quick, but couldn't stay mad watching Aretha non-glare back at her. Aretha was an unexpected gift sent from heaven and Jennifer knew it. Seeing Ian so happy was proof of that. She relaxed.

"I love you too, Jennifer," Aretha said solemnly.

Jennifer stared at Aretha starting to get used to the fact that Aretha was clairvoyant. Ian had taken a step back and crossed his arms letting Aretha do what she did best—give love and give it good. Jennifer finally admitted, "I can't believe I just met you and you can have this effect on me," she poked a look at Ian, then Aretha, "…us."

All Aretha said was. "Please be careful."

"I certainly will," Jennifer looked at the cargo ramp.

Sami pulled back from giving Dimitri a goodbye hug, then watched as he jogged down the ramp stopping next to Channing to reach for the joystick controller.

"I'll take it from here, Channing."

Channing nodded and handed Dimitri the controller.

Dimitri looked at Jennifer, "You almost ready, my Lord?"

"Yes, just waiting—" Jennifer smiled seeing Krachy approach with Parent following a few steps behind him. Jennifer swung her arms around Krachy and eyed Parent behind him as she untangled.

Krachy pushed Jennifer back at arm's length searching her eyes.

"Don't get pinched again."

"I won't, right, Parent?" Jennifer held onto Krachy's hand looking at Parent expectantly.

"You won't, Amanda and Richard are set up and waiting. I promise they'll do their job."

"Good enough for me," Jennifer dropped her grip and moved to the latch on the livestock container door on one end. She dogged the latch, pulled it open, and instructed, "Carol and Lan need about 15 minutes to set up, Dimitri. We can take our time getting there." Her head swiveled to Parent.

Parent knew what Jennifer was going to ask before she asked it.

"Not yet, Jennifer. Maddy hasn't made a move to dismantle any of my operations or I would have heard about it. Of course, that could change at any minute."

This was a key part of what Maddy was planning—very key.

Jennifer let out the breath she was holding. A lot hinged on timing at this point. If Maddy started to dismantle Parent's operations before she arrived at the man's apartment, that would mean something very important. The thing it meant was not a showstopper per se, but it would determine how the rest of Jennifer's plan played out. Jennifer had briefed everyone on the team about either contingency.

Parent dipped his head,"You should go then."

Jennifer bent down and duck walked into the container. Dimitri closed the swinging door and latched it.

Channing opened the blast hatch and stood aside as Dimitri powered up the anti-grav container guiding it out onto the shipping concourse street. The hatch closed behind him.

There was still over 10 minutes left before Carol and Lan would be in position. The foot traffic was light but steady on the shipping concourse street. The livestock container didn't look out of place among the other anti-grav shipping containers being led along by other people moving their goods down the wide street. Jennifer's intention was to blend in with the sparse crowd at this hour. For example, it wasn't uncommon for people to leave their containers powered down outside an eatery while the driver went in for a bite to eat.

Dimitri insisted on being Jennifer's escort. There was no argument from Jennifer. She wanted Dimitri with her. Their kinship bond was genetic for Dimitri. He had sworn fealty to Jennifer years prior and been her vassal ever since. He would protect her life with his own— non-failing, absolute.

Dimitri swiveled his head hearing a small pack of Station Security guards jog up from behind him. Their dura body armor suit servos grew in volume until the fast approaching pack dodged Dimitri and his container heading down the street ahead. Dimitri didn't tense or give an indication that a wanted fugitive was inside the container he drove. He just stayed his course.

The last Sta Sec guard in the formation turned abruptly holding up a hand signaling Dimitri.

"Stop, re-route!" The man ordered. The Sta Sec guards up ahead disbursed and lined up single file jogging one-by-one into an alley between two shops.

Dimitri did as he was told. All the Sta Sec guard wanted was for him to re-route his container as to not interfere with the raid the guards were obviously going to perform down the alleyway. Dimitri eyed an eatery on the opposite side of the street and guided the container next to the entrance then powered it down next to the few tables and chairs arranged on the sidewalk in front of the diner.

The last of the Sta Sec guards disappeared in the alleyway. In no time the guards had made their arrests. The alley led to a massage parlor and the older mama-san plus two young ethnic looking ladies were in tie-wrap cuffs being led from the alley. The three women looked tired like they had been rousted awake. They were questioned briefly. The Sta Sec lead guard, a sergeant, tried to question the three women but all they did was shake their heads, not saying a word.

Jennifer watched through one of the air holes and knew why the women were so rigidly close-lipped.

"Their oath-sworn, Dimitri," she whispered.

"They're sworn to Parent, my Lord. Correct?"

Dimitri couldn't see Jennifer nod, "Yep. Unfortunately, Sta Sec has already started to dismantle the VG. I still want to grab the man from his apartment just like we planned. Maddy is already using her advantage to start dismantling the VG from the ground up just like Parent and I discussed."

This seemingly minor arrest was just more proof for Jennifer's theory on how the woman Maddy was going to take over Biltmire Space Station, and that Maddy intended to do it fast using the space station's own law enforcement force to do her dirty work for her.

The timing was faster than even Jennifer could have anticipated, but that was okay. Jennifer was nothing if not adaptable.

"I'll have to wait a little while longer to prove my innocence," Jennifer reasoned, "but this arrest just proves Maddy is moving fast and has already made the switch."

The Sta Sec guards cleared out in short order escorting their prisoners away. The scene across the street looked untouched, as if nothing had taken place.

Dimitri powered up the container and eased the joystick forward toward the target apartment. The apartment he and Jennifer were heading for was on the second floor in the residential concourse. Dimitri scanned the concourse street in both directions and saw nothing out of the ordinary. Getting the anti-grav container up to the second floor would be easy. Dimitri took a lift tube leaving the container on the ground floor concourse, looked over the second floor balcony, then urged the joy controller higher guiding the large container up then over the balcony railing.

The target apartment was just ahead on the right. Dimitri powered down the container. Abandoning cover, Jennifer jumped out once Dimitri opened the swinging door. Jennifer walked purposefully over to the apartment hatch, a shiver of tension creeping up her spine. Amanda and Richard were close by. Parent had assured her they would be. But now, their services would not be needed—The person that would open the hatch WAS NOT the real Commander of Biltmire Station Security. Jennifer trying to prove her innocence to this imposter using Amanda and Richard's help would be useless. However, the imposter was not useless himself. Not at all… Jennifer thumbed the door comm above the scan pad.

After a minute a man's voice answered through the commo.

"Yeah, the hell you want at this hour?"

Jennifer launched right in.

"I'm Jennifer Bane. I'm wanted for murder and attempted kidnapping. I'm here to turn myself in. You have about 15 seconds before I change my mind and leave!" The volume of her confession was loud by design. Jennifer wanted Carol and Lan to hear it. The two of them should already be in position via their route from under-deck.

After about 10 seconds the hatch started to move aside, a laser pistol the first thing visible in the widening gap of the hatch. No sooner than the hatch was fully open, a massive tackle slammed the faux head of station security from behind. The laser pistol tumbled from the man's grip. Dimitri already had the shipping container door open accepting the stunned captive like the jaws of a shark stretching its mouth open to accept its next meal.

Carol then Lan hopped off the stunned man's surprised body inside the container and crawled out fast. Jennifer bent down, picked up the LP, fingered the setting switch to NL mode, then pumped not one, but two laser bolts dead center into the right then the left butt cheek of the imposter. In Non-Lethal mode the weapon didn't kill, only stun. The man didn't make a sound. He was shocked hard by the energy bolt cracks, out cold.

Jennifer looked at Carol.

"How'd you know not to wait for Amanda and Richard to do their thing?"

Carol lifted her chin, "Look behind you."

Jennifer spun and saw the married couple standing next to the balcony railing and turned back to Carol.

Carol explained, "I spotted them standing there when the hatch started to open and figured that since I *did* see them they weren't gonna intervene."

Lan reached out for Carol's neck caressing it in FF connect. Lan smiled.

"Good call, Carol." Lan waited a few more seconds before she removed her grip.

"So we got what we need here, right?" Carol glanced distastefully at the shipping container then back at Jennifer.

"We do!" Jennifer dipped her head once. "I don't wanna climb back inside that thing with that guy."

Before Jennifer could react, be surprised, or even register the wind on her face, her eyes started watering. Jennifer quickly figured out that she was being carried through the space station. Confused, even shocked, she just shut her eyes tight. The feeling was unnatural yet safe for some reason. Her neck was not being jerked sideways with each violent change in direction. How the heck was that possible? The warmth on either side of Jennifer's head was very noticeable. The wind rippling the skin on her face was cool but the vice-like heat over each ear and side of her head was warm, firm. Then the wind stopped. When Jennifer opened her eyes she was standing in Parent's landing bay in front of the closed blast hatch behind her.

Jennifer blinked, breathing hard but with no noxious pain in her head at all.

Parent pulled his eyebrows together.

"I told them your head needed extra care. You okay?"

Jennifer looked side-to-side seeing Amanda and Richard ease her from their grasp.

Krachy slipped an arm around Jennifer's waist; with his other hand he wiped at a few tears on her face with a tissue. "You missed the best part."

"I—I kept my eyes closed," Jennifer stammered.

"Scared about your head, I understand."

"No, yes, I don't know, just scared altogether!"

"Nothing to be afraid of, Jennifer," Parent assured her.

Jennifer looked at Amanda, "I guess I should thank you for getting me back here without being seen. The guy we captured is not the head of Station Security. He's a fake. I'm sure of it. But if another Sta Sec guard saw me on my way back here it could have been a problem. Thanks."

"You're welcome," Amanda answered.

Jennifer looked at Krachy.

Krachy reassured her, "You seem pretty sure about this plan of yours. I wanna see it for myself. Should be interesting."

"As soon as the imposter gets here I'll show you," Jennifer took in the others around her with her eyes. "I'll show all of you."

Parent's forehead knotted, "How are you going to show us he's an imposter, Jennifer?"

Jennifer crinkled her lips. "Trust me. I only shot the bastard in the ass. Wait until I light up his neck. I know about the ACTs, the accelerated computer tissues, and how they work. A good jolt in the neck with an LP in NL mode should do the trick."

SEVENTEEN

Fifteen minutes later Dimitri guided the anti grav shipping container in through the blast hatch. Everyone standing expectantly on the other side shuffled back to let Dimitri bring it through and power it down in the large landing bay. Carol and Lan walked purposefully out the maintenance room hatch and wiped at their faces with towels coming to a stop near Dimitri.

So far, the only thing everyone had was Jennifer's theory that the guy they'd just captured would prove her plan on how Maddy was going to take over Biltmire Space Station was right.

Not wasting any time, Jennifer dove in.

"Maddy discovered a new way to use the accelerated computer tissues. When Murphy brought back the small container of ACTs from the booty heist on-station I wondered why there we so many of them. Then, once I understood how the ACTs could be used as a haptic device, I started thinking. At that point things started to move fast and the next thing I know I was on Cimmerian Space Lab," Jennifer glanced over at Amanda.

Amanda nodded as she addressed the others.

"Jennifer pulled me aside and had me explain how I can do what I do. How I have this incredible speed in my legs. I explained that the only way my body can stand up to the rigors of using the nano-machines is to implant accelerated computer tissues in each leg that control the pain. I told Jennifer about how the ACTs acted like a haptic device. The haptics provide electrical nerve feedback to my brain that say I'm not in pain.

The haptics also allow my brain to receive sensations of touch and feeling in my legs…" Amanda trailed off, her approving look landing on Jennifer.

"That's when I put it all together. After what I saw, and rescued, off Cimmerian, I then knew that Maddy had more plans for the ACTs. Maddy was not only using them for speed, using them for stealth. Maddy figured out at least one other use for them—"

The faux Station Security detainee in the container roused and moaned. Jennifer glanced at Dimitri with a look only he could decipher. He pulled the laser pistol out of his pocket, opened the door on the container, and popped a white hot bolt of energy into the guy's ass. The man jerked like he'd been stabbed in the butt with a spear, then deflated returning to sleepy land once again.

"…As your were explaining, my Lord…" Dimitri nodded an apology for the brief interruption.

"Let's do one thing before I show everyone how I know this man is an imposter, Dimitri. Can you pull him out of the container for me?" Dimitri did as he was asked, at the same time Jennifer looked at Nace.

"Nace, you're now going to be the captain in charge of Biltmire Space Station Detention. Can you come close so I can get this man's finger print ID and yours to confirm this advancement in promotion?"

Nace hesitated, scrunching her forehead, clearly puzzled. This guy was an imposter wasn't he?

Murphy moved up to Nace's side and grabbed her wrist.

"Go ahead, Nace." She urged her to move closer toward the unconscious man who looked just like the head of Sta Sec, a man named Alton Myatt. Dimitri already had fake Myatt out of the container lying sprawled on the deck. Dimitri roughly pulled at the imposter's hand directing his thumb toward the scan screen on Murphy's hand comp.

"You go first, Nace," Murphy held the scan pad out in front of Nace, dipped her eyes down at it, then back at Nace.

When Nace hesitated Jennifer reassured her, "Krachy said you were going to run detention when this whole thing was over. There is always room at the top. I would never tell you there is not. Your promotion takes effect now, if that's okay with you, captain?"

The grin on Jennifer's lips was insidious.

Nace rippled and twitched her lips, then the doubtful look on her face changed as the corners of her mouth rose into an underhanded grin of her own.

"Captain, I like the sound of that." She pressed her thumb on the scan pad, it chirped. Nace held back a smile while she waited for the *finger of fate* from the imposter to confirm the change that would redirect the path of her life aboard the *annoyed train* straight onto the *yes, we can do train* with the next chirp of the hand comp. Nace was now liking this team-work shit a lot, for sure, and couldn't help planting a cat's grin on Krachy. Krachy had his arms folded across his chest beaming a full-on crooked Krachy smile.

Murphy pressed the imposters thumb to the scan pad, the *yes, we can do* chirp sounded like a loud clap of thunder in Nace's ears. Nace's face seemed to shed years of hard stress she carried with her like a curtana jabbing her happiness into submission. A fine glow of color permeated Nace's not-so-hollow cheeks and she crossed her arms, smiling strong, anticipating what was next.

Jennifer nodded at Dimitiri, the two of them on the exact same genetic wavelength. Everyone else looked on without a word.

Dimitri reached in a pocket and pulled out a set of tweezers. Holding the thumb of the imposter in his hand he pinched at the base of the trickster's limp thumb, the thumb that had just caused the chirp, pulling back a thin layer of transparent film from its surface. He held it in the teeth of the tweezers for everyone to see as he explained.

"My Lord asked Nace to recon detention to get the names, but most importantly the physical descriptions, of the people Maddy snagged from detention. The man we have here matches the description of Alton Myatt, the real head of Biltmire Station Security. Maddy kidnapped the *real* Alton Myatt so that he could be replaced with this man. This man is a prisoner serving a rather long sentence for attempted murder. The film I pulled from his thumb matches the thumb print of Alton Myatt." Dimitri peered at his lord letting her finish.

Jennifer continued, "Maddy had the nurse that used to work in detention help her implant accelerated computer tissues in this guy's jaw and neck. In addition, to make it even more believable, she had each of this man's fingers fitted with a form of synthetic skin that holds the same finger prints as Alton Myatt's fingers. The reason why this man's face looks like Alton Myatt is because Maddy has developed yet another 'categorization' use for the accelerated computer tissues. Dimitri, hand me your laser pistol."

Dimitri passed it over to her.

"Watch this." Jennifer grabbed the LP, and after making sure it was in Non-Lethal mode, went down on one knee, then placed the barrel tip of the weapon just under the jawline of the fake leader. She squeezed off a quick jolt.

The affect was immediate and increased in speed building rapidly. The man's head jerked sideways from the short blast, then the transformation started in the man's jaw first. The man's jaw began to quake side-to-side. His jaw looked like a cow working his cud but on steroids. Fast, then faster, then blindingly fast the man's jaw shivered so hard side-to-side that his whole head quivered in a ferocious, gyrating velocity that blurred the pulsating tempo. The mouth, then the cheeks, then the forehead joined in on the wicked-quick trembling oscillation shaking the man's face so fast it wasn't visible until it stopped dead. The only thing that revealed anything had changed on the man's face was a line of drool leaking out one side of his mouth AND that his face was not that of Alton Myatt any longer.

Murphy handed her hand comp to Jennifer. Jennifer turned the small screen to her audience. When she spoke she looked at Nace.

"The ACTs were implanted in his neck and jaw. This man is Blanny Jane, Nace. Jane was taken from detention by Maddy to impersonate the head of Biltmire Station Security Alton Myatt. Or, Maddy just offered Jane the job, doesn't really matter. Jane was serving a long sentence. My guess is he accepted Maddy's offer and found it easy to *commit to the bit.*"

Nace squinted at the picture on the HC. It was Blanny Jane's picture. The same face now rested atop the unconscious body on the deck at Dimitri's feet.

Jennifer continued, "Maddy found a way to program the ACT's to impersonate someone's face. She added the fake fingerprints to complete the charade."

Nace eyed Jennifer looking for more.

Jennifer nodded, "That's why your recon was so important, Nace. Right, Murphy?" She turned to Murphy.

"That's right," Murphy continued. "The physical description of Blanny Jane matches Alton Myatt, or at least so close no one could tell them apart physically, especially since Maddy reprogrammed Jane's implanted ACTs with Myatt's facial features." Murphy smirked. "Heady stuff, eh, Nace?" Her eyelids arched at the play on words.

A side of Nace's mouth turned up, "Quite heady, yes." Nace looked at Krachy, "How did you know you could put me in charge of detention, Krachy? You knew about his face-mask stuff when you told me to run things after all this was over?"

Krachy shook his head.

"Nope, had no idea. I just know the kind of company I keep, Nace." He eyeballed Jennifer.

Nace clocked a look Jennifer's way too.

"Being a captain is mighty, Jennifer." Nace looked pleased.

Jennifer smiled, "There's no shame to my game, Nace. I didn't do this to get on your good side. Even though I NEVER want to be on the receiving end of one of your artillery shells again!" Jennifer rubbed the sore spot on her chest. "I'd like to think you won't let something like this happen again, now that you've seen how evil people can be when they pervert technology the wrong way. We're good on that, you and I, right?"

Nace knew what Jennifer meant by that last question. This situation was much bigger than Nace's past hate for Jennifer and the whip-ass in Carol's cell a few short days ago. There was a renewed responsibility here. That responsibility showed. Nace pulled in a rasping inhalation; her shoulders swelled. She nodded once, a shared understanding thick in the air between the two women. A long-delayed connection lit up Nace's brain. There was no lingering animosity toward Jennifer now. Just duty...

"So, you had to get this guy's fingerprint to confirm my promotion because, basically, this imposter really is Alton Myatt right now....right?"

Jennifer nodded.

"Hey, I'm not going to say that the real Myatt didn't give you the promo if you don't. Besides, I'm not so sure where the real Alton Myatt is. I hope Maddy didn't kill him, but I don't know that to be the case one way or another."

Krachy looked at Jennifer.

"You said that I would understand Maddy's plan once you showed me this and I saw the people you rescued off Cimmerian Space Lab. I haven't seen the people you rescue—"

Aretha interrupted. "—I have, or no, I haven't actually seen them. But I know what Jennifer is talking about, Krachy. I felt what was left of their faces..." Aretha reached for Ian's hand beside her, like she was reaching for a rampart to stand up to all the hurt in her life now that her eyes were gone, or to seek closure, no one could tell.

Maybe Ian knew.

"Are you okay telling us about this, sweetie?" Ian's voice was thick with concern.

Aretha shifted her non-gaze on Ian.

"I told Jennifer when I first talked to her alone that she may as well accept the fact that I'm a part of this. You supporting me is all the fuel I need." She managed a weak smile.

"Go ahead, then."

Aretha rotated her face toward where Krachy was standing.

"Krachy, the Chancellor of Cimmerian was performing experiments on the faces of several of my friends. The result of the experiments left what I can only term as post-stroke victims."

Parent bobbed his head up-and-down rubbing at his chin, finally understanding the need for assisted living and skilled nursing. He looked at Jennifer.

"The Cimmerian victims had their faces wiped, Jennifer?"

Jennifer's lips thinned. She spoke slowly in an attempt to restrain her mounting anger so the explanation would be crystal clear to everyone, not just Parent.

"I'm glad Aretha hasn't seen what I have, Parent. Maddy paid the Chancellor to test the ACTs on some of Aretha's friends. The results deactivated the muscles and nerves in four of the people's faces. One of the most important components of our faces is the fat that lies just beneath the skin. Fat accentuates parts of our face to make it distinct to, well, to you, to each of us. The experiments made the fat in the four people not just shrink—the fat congealed. I don't know how to explain it, but the fat solidified, joined with, the ligaments and tendons that provide support to the soft tissues of the face. These four people can no longer use the ligaments and tendons that provide points for movement of muscles and facial expressions."

Jennifer swallowed. "Four people no longer have a face that shows identity or emotion. The face on these four people is hard like, like, a full facial callous."

Aretha nodded. "My friends have hard skin where their faces used to be. And their eyelids don't have any way to lift so they're blind just like me. The dead hardened skin over each eye is snapped shut blocking their vision."

Ian squeezed her hand gently. Aretha non-stared at Ian, her breath picking up speed.

"Ian, my eyes were taken to be used to create some sort of super-vision using the ACTs." She guided her voice along dura steel rails. Then Aretha's head swung toward Jennifer.

"Speed, stealth, face duplication, and with my eyes— enhanced vision. Sight beyond that of other humans. Maddy was expanding her market not just enhancing people with speed, stealth, and face replication. She also wants to sell people enhanced with super sight too."

Jennifer looked at Parent.

"Maddy had Blanny Jane start dismantling your operation, Parent. On the way to capture him, Dimitri and I saw Station Security raid one of your massage parlors."

Parent nodded knowing what this meant.

"That's why Amanda and Richard weren't needed."

Carol added, "I saw Amanda and Richard standing behind Jennifer before we tackled Blanny Jane into the shipping container." She looked at Jennifer. "You were going to have Amanda and Richard put on a show to help prove your innocence....that will have to wait, won't it, Jennifer?"

Jennifer frowned.

"Once I saw that Sta Sec was starting to dismantle Parent's operation, I knew Alton Myatt was an imposter. All along Maddy intended to use Station Security to do her dirty work by planting Blanny Jane in Myatt's place. Maddy essentially controlled Station Security with the imposter in place. She ordered Jane, in his role as the fake Sta Sec leader, to start dismantling Parent's operations. Amanda and Richard WOULD have helped me prove I didn't kill or kidnap anyone during the riot..."

Amanda pulled out a laser blade from her pocket.

"I was going to use my speed to place this laser blade into Jennifer's hand if Alton Myatt was really himself. Once the hatch opened to Myatt's apartment, Jennifer was going to tell Myatt to watch closely. I would have inserted the weapon into Jennifer's hand so that Myatt could see how Jennifer was framed during the riot using speed. Of course, since Blanny Jane had already been switched for Myatt, that wasn't possible."

Jennifer took in a breath.

"I just have to wait until I'm in front of a tribunal judge to prove I'm innocent. Amanda'll be in the courtroom and will perform the same theatrics for the judge as she would have for the real Alton Myatt. Also—" Jennifer eyed Murphy.

Murphy's look hardened.

"I have a copy of the Station Security video surveillance camera taken during the riot that shows the moment Jennifer was framed by one of Maddy's speed minions. Jennifer helped pull a little boy out of the path of a laser blade. I obtained the vid footage that shows what happened. Once Jennifer shows the judge that vid footage and Amanda performs her speedy theatrics in the courtroom, Jennifer should be cleared of any wrongdoing."

Lan spoke fast, one of her feet tapping rapidly.

"But you have to wait, Jennifer. You have to prove your innocence in front of a judge. That means..."

Jennifer attempted to wave off Lan's concern with a careless hand, but anxiety made her throat clinch. She cleared her throat, managing a weak smile, "You're right, Lan."

Lan's head jerked toward Krachy with a look that said, *How can you let this happen!*

"You're not serious! Please tell me you're not going to go through with this!"

Jennifer eased an apprehensive arm around her Short Man Hunk like she always did when she needed reassurance that everything would be okay.

"It takes bravery to do the right thing, Lan. Right, Carol?" One of Jennifer's eyelids inched up but she couldn't manage to lift the same corner of her mouth. The beginnings of a smile was just not possible at the moment.

Carol pressed a hand onto Lan's wrist, squeezing. Lan turned to look at Carol.

"Trust her, Lan. She's got this." Carol's grin was devious.

Despite Jennifer's derring-do, she was scared stiff about what she intended to do. Jennifer was going to turn herself into Sta Sec Detention and be judged for the crimes she did not commit. That was what was bothering Lan so much. Lan knew Jennifer was going to let herself be arrested and thrown into detention to face her fate. Jennifer tried to square her shoulders, but the quickening heartbeat in her ears, each thump distinct, caused her to swallow and second guess this screwball plan.

Sami, nowhere to be seen until now, suddenly came bounding down the cargo ramp. She made her way unsteadily over to Jennifer's side.

Jennifer surveyed what Sami had in each hand, her eyes finally landing on Sami's smile. A nameless dread spilled over Jennifer thinking that Sami was happy to see Jennifer turn herself in with no guarantee of clemency once behind bars.

Sami burped. "Just getting a head start," then threw back another swig of her cocktail. She handed the bottle in her other hand to Dimitri. "You need to catch up, Big D," Sami giggled letting Dimitri grab the open bottle and rifle down a gulp himself.

My own vassal! Jennifer thought to herself. Her bones turned to jelly at the callousness of Dimitri joining in to celebrate his lord's upcoming trip back to detention.

Carol had about all she could take of Jennifer's pity party, stepped over, shot a hand through Jennifer's free arm, and pulled her away from Krachy through the already open blast hatch.

"Calm down. I told you before not to go throwin' a wobbly. Your friends haven't deserted you. Chill!"

Jennifer let herself be pulled through the hatch out onto the concourse street. She walked in a fog of confusion, searching Carol's face for an answer.

Carol smiled, "I'm going with you, Jennifer. Relax. I only have two weeks left on my sentence, plus the escape time whatever that'll be. Besides," Carol looked back over her shoulder as Nace came up behind the two women, then back into Jennifer's hurt eyes, "after all you've done for me and Biltmire, I wouldn't miss what's coming next for nothin'."

Nace grabbed Jennifer's other arm roughly. Jennifer twisted her neck fast to catch a fleeting glimpse of Krachy taking a pull on the bottle as the hatch slide shut.

Jennifer's eyes darted from left-to-right no longer struggling to conceal her shock that even her fiancé, the man that promised to marry her, seemed to be celebrating too! Jennifer opened her mouth, but shock prevented the gobsmacked words of protest from forming on her lips.

As Carol and Nace's grips tightened pulling Jennifer along making a beeline in the direction of detention, Carol leaned forward looking past Jennifer at Nace, and said with satisfaction, "I swear this is the first time Jennifer's been speechless. The silence is blissful, don't you think?"

"I know, right?" Nace snorted, "Probably won't last long."

The uncaring words Jennifer was hearing took time to register. By then, Nace was already reaching out pushing the comm button above the detention intake scan pad.

"Prisoner intake, two," Nace said authoritatively.

Jennifer blinked, bewildered.

"I…I don't want to do this. I don't! Really, I don't want to go through with this now!"

"Told you," Nace shook her head and shoved Jennifer through the open hatch followed by Carol. The hatch closed.

EIGHTEEN

A lone tear formed in Jennifer's eye. She sat alone in the same interrogation room Nace Notchins had put her in when she was arrested during the riot several days ago. Jennifer hugged herself and tried to think. *There had to be a reason her sworn vassal toasted her re-arrest, Sami too. There had to be a reason Krachy joined in, just had to be!*

But Jennifer was tired. Fear and confusion had worn her out, and her earlier euphoria of exposing Maddy's evil plan had died with a shattering crash. A crash that was assisted by people she thought loved her. Worst still, the bitch Maddy was still at large. Not that Jennifer could do much about that now—

The hatch opened, and the tear dripped down Jennifer's cheek when she lifted her head.

"It can't be," Jennifer whispered.

In time, the child's life she saved would be what she remembered, not the bloodied body on the deck.

Nace stuck her head around the hatch frame.

"Five minutes visitation, prisoner Bane."

Jennifer had never seen how white Nace's teeth were, but they beamed out a delighted smile now. Hollow Cheeks looked like a different person.

"My wedding present to you," Nace said to Jennifer, then gently pushed at the back of the little boy. "It's okay, Adam. Jennifer was the lady that helped you a few days ago."

Adam, the little boy Jennifer had saved the life of during the riot, pushed a fingernail to his teeth nibbling as he looked up at Nace, then back at Jennifer seated on the other side of the small table.

Jennifer controlled her astonishment, forcing her elation to hang back. Before she could cast her thankful eyes on Nace, the hatch closed.

Adam reached into his trouser pocket and pulled out a little toy soldier, a space commando mini-figure. He stepped up to the table and placed it in front of Jennifer.

"The arm is missing." His round, trusting eyes, pierced Jennifer's soul. Despite herself, she gasped. Jennifer eyed his other trouser pocket.

"Is the arm in there, in your other pocket maybe?"

She asked as gently as she could given she was about to explode with joy.

Adam dug deep in his pocket for what seemed like a minute but was really only five seconds. His eyes lit up lifting what he'd found.

"How'd you know?" He gripped the small snap-on arm and handed it to Jennifer's outstretched hand as she came around the table going down on one knee beside him.

Adam was focused on the piece in Jennifer's hand. Jennifer couldn't help but let out a giddy breath.

"Here, I think I can snap it back on. That'll make your little commando happy again." She snapped the arm on the commando's shoulder and held it up looking it over. "That looks better. What'd you think?"

"Lemme see," Adam grabbed it from Jennifer and nodded. "Gotta name him." His soft blue eyes searched Jennifer's face. "Johnny, I like Johnny. Kinda sounds like Jennifer. But he's a boy, so I say, Johnny."

Jennifer smiled fighting a near unrestrained urge to pull Adam against her chest and squeeze the life right out of the boy. The hatch opened behind them.

Adam turned holding up the commando with pride.

"Jennifer fixed him!"

Nace smiled warmly, "She fixes lots of stuff, Adam."

Adam turned back to Jennifer.

"I'm gonna come back to see you when somethin' else breaks."

Jennifer stood.

"Can't wait, Adam."

Adam smiled. Nace guided a caring hand to the back of Adam's head nudging him past her and out through the hatch. Nace twisted watching him leave then swung her haughty look back at Jennifer.

"There's more. Wanna see?"

Jennifer's heart pounded and she was juiced with adrenaline, happiness, and uncertainty all at once. She exhaled.

"Nothing is more than Adam, Nace."

"I beg to differ, twice."

Jennifer's brow knitted.

Nace pulled a laser pistol from her pocket and jerked her head out the hatch motioning Jennifer to follow.

The fear and confusion that enveloped Jennifer had, to some degree, left the interrogation room pulled effortlessly out of the hatch when Adam left. Jennifer strode after Nace following fast on her heels.

Station time was just after 5:30am. All the prisoners were asleep, the detention center strangely silent compared to Jennifer's last visit during the riot.

Nace stopped up ahead at a cell hatch on the second floor and pressed the comm.

"Open two ten."

The hatch slid aside. Asleep on the bottom bunk was a woman, her fast, loud, breathing clearly audible as Nace stepped up to her.

"Wakey, wakey, eggs and bakey!"

The woman roused, blinked back sleep.

Before the woman's eyes registered Nace standing over her, Nace plunged the tip of the LP barrel into the underside of the woman's jaw squeezing off a quick bolt.

Zint!

The woman's head jerked back straining her neck muscles tense. Her face turned to quivering rubber with a rapidity only matched by Jennifer's full-tilt look of pure amazement at what was happening in front of her. The woman's face shuddered side-to-side in a blurring frenzy smacking her jaws together with a blubbering, wet, gurgle. Then the hurricane stopped.

Resting atop the woman's unconscious shoulders was the face of Stone-Face-Lady. None other than the crafty bitch responsible for everything—Maddy.

Seeing Maddy on the bunk in a detention cell was a huge relief for Jennifer. But at the same time she was stupefied why Krachy, Sami, and Dimitri had hurt her. Jennifer was riding a dazed wave of indecision when Carol poked her head around the hatch jamb.

"That Maddy?" Carol asked Nace, brushing past the two women to stand over Maddy.

"Uh-huh," Nace folded her arms over her chest.

Carol bent down over Maddy, face twisted.

"Bee-Utch!" She yelled, then rifled both hands to either side of Maddy's face slapping her cheeks rapidly back-and-forth for several seconds before straitening to look at Nace.

"Feel better?" Nace asked.

"Much!"

Jennifer tried to smile, but it faltered.

"What's going on here?" She managed.

Carol looked to Nace expectantly who said, "When you went to capture Blanny Jane, I spoke with Krachy. He and I worked it all out."

"Worked what out?"

"Hey, you told to me that I shouldn't let something like this happen again, now that I've seen how evil people can be when they pervert technology the wrong way. So I just thought it through. I was convinced I could find a solution and the solution found me. What better place for Maddy to hole up but in detention, Jennifer? Maddy can't get off-station. Not with your three-starship blockade stopping and searching every ship that leaves Biltmire local space. Maddy gave Blanny Jane all the orders he needed when they were both here in detention together. Then Blanny Jane left detention, but Maddy stayed here.

"Krachy told me you would never fall for anything like *starting with detention*. You were convinced that Maddy had moved on, to plan her next set of moves. Well, you did fall for Maddy's misdirection in a way, Jennifer. You thought that Maddy had moved on quickly and left detention, but she never did. Only her minion Blanny Jane did, you know, to carry out Maddy's orders to take over the space station as the new fake head of Station Security. Once the takeover was well on its way, Blanny Jane would have gotten Maddy released."

"You and Krachy figured all this out while I was capturing Blanny Jane?"

Nace hacked a snort, not intentionally; her nose still hurt like hell. She looked at Carol.

Carol shook her head responding to Nace.

"Jennifer just can't believe she's not always right. She thinks she's a spellbinder, to a fault." Carol eyed Jennifer, jibed, "Roll with it, Jennifer." Carol was loving that she and Nace were the ones that surprised Jennifer.

Jennifer regarded both women, examining the pieces from different angles, weighing them, shuffling them, trying to decide which ones she could get to cohere. There was only one piece Jennifer could not understand—the perceived betrayal of her fiancé and friends formed on her lips as a question that had to be answered.

"But—" Jennifer started.

"—Turn around will you?" Carol lifted her chin looking behind Jennifer.

Jennifer spun around.

Krachy, Dimitri, and Sami stood just outside the cell hatch, the two detention guards behind them looking expectantly at Nace.

Nace instructed, "Pull the tie wraps off the two men."

The two guards did as they were told, releasing Krachy and Dimitri's wrists, then took a few steps back waiting for their next order. Nace stepped out of the cell up behind Sami to undo her wrists.

The three new detainees looked like they had been in a fist fight. Krachy's upper lip was swelled pulling the side of his mouth high up his cheek forming a lopsided grimace. Sami had a few drops of blood drying under a nostril; she held a sore arm across her stomach. Dimitri had the beginnings of a shiner under one bloodshot eye.

Sami belched.

Jennifer could smell the liquor strong on her breath.

Sami slurred, "Doubwool?"

Jennifer gathered in the battered trio, not able to parse the shit running through her bewildered mind, but opened her mouth anyway.

"What did you say?"

Krachy stepped forward.

"She asked double, love. Get it, double, you know…double?" Krachy snickered, looked at Nace. "Can you help her, Nacey?"

Jennifer wheeled her stare at Nace. "Nacey?"

Nace blew a sniff out a nostril.

"For shit's sake, Jennifer, I've known Krachy a lot longer than you. He always used to call me that at the academy, just to piss me off. But now, it's kinda cute, in a drunk, Krachy's-not-a-fiancé-much-longer sorta way."

"…Not longer *what* way?"

Carol could not believe Jennifer was this slow on the uptake and laughed.

"Will you just hold out your thumb, Bane!"

When Jennifer hesitated, Nace grabbed Jennifer's thumb and pressed it to the hand comp screen in her hand.

"The tribunal probate court just needs Krachy's thumb-print before your marriage is official."

Nace turned to Krachy already extending his thumb. Nace grabbed his thumb and the hand comp chirped when the thumbprint hit home.

Jennifer still held out her hand tentatively, the fact that Krachy and her were married only now beginning to register, although at a glacial pace, on Jennifer's face. She looked on as Sami then Dimitri pressed their thumbs in turn to the scan pad. Marriages had to be registered with tribunal probate court to be legal. Nace's hand comp app was piped directly into probate court.

Krachy looped an arm through Jennifer's elbow.

"The three of us were just arrested for drunk and disorderly conduct. I'm freakin' locked!" He covered a hiccup with his hand. "I got an extra charge for resisting arrest."

Jennifer FINALLY understood that Adam, Maddy, and the marriage were joined together. That the three feats were all tied up into a ball, gift wrapped for her by her friends and fiancé.

"Oh my God!" Jennifer smiled. "You three got thrown in here so that we could perform the doubwool marriage?"

"Of course, my Lord," Dimitri confirmed, face flush. "All of us talked about this right after I proposed to Sami. Krachy said you wanted a doubwool." He swallowed back a belch. "So we drank up and picked a fight with each outher in front of a few Sta Sec guards so we'd get tossed in here with you."

Something like awe came over Jennifer's face.

"And you, Nace, you had Adam visit me, as a gift?"

"Hey, I'm just returning the favor, Jennifer. Sort of like a *Return Delivery*. You delivered a way to stop Maddy. I delivered Adam to show my thanks."

Nace eyed Sami, Dimitri, and Krachy.

"Now I'm going to deliver the marriage ceremony. As captain, I have the authority." She peered at Jennifer. "You made sure of that."

Jennifer turned to Krachy, "What about the honeymoon, love?"

"That's why I took the extra charge," Krachy grinned crookedly.

"I have to stay behind bars a bit longer…"

EPILOGUE

"Do I have to spell it out or what?! I said you are EXONERATED!" The hot-tempered tribunal judge scowled at Jennifer from behind her desk in the spacious courtroom adjacent to Biltmire Detention.

Jennifer's lips tightened into a frown refusing to open her big mouth again. She was getting cleared of her criminal charges of murder and attempted kidnapping and didn't want to blow it now that she was so close.

Good choice.

"Yeah, that's what I thought. You've caused enough trouble already." The middle-aged woman threw the back of her hand to her mouth covering a yawn. Station time was just past 6:30am. Newly christened Captain Nace Notchins had insisted that Judge Furman hold court now instead of waiting until Furman's usual start time of 9:30am. *This*, Captain Notchins had explained, couldn't wait. Amanda, Jennifer and Nace were the only ones in the courtroom.

Judge Furman eyed Amanda, the target of her focused annoyance just now. Annoyance that bristled the corners of Furman's lips and dripped from every word she barked.

"If you do that bluring-knees-bent-running-around-thing ONE MORE TIME a fat charge of contempt of court is comin' your way! One second you're standing way over there next to the entry hatch without my hand comp in your hand, then a split second later my HC is in your hand! I'm not pretending to know how that's possible."

Amanda dipped her head sheepishly then placed the judge's hand comp back down on the desk. She had just walked

213

SLOWLY back over to the judge's desk returning the property that wasn't hers for a second time.

Judge Furman narrowed her brown eyes watchfully inspecting each movement of Amanda's hand until the hand comp rested in its original place.

Furman adressed Jennifer.

"For the record, Jennifer Bane: You are hereby cleared of the charges of murder and attempted kidnapping based on the vid footage you provided that clearly shows some weird phenomenon Amanda just seemed to demonstrate where a laser blade miraculously ended up in your hand after you saved the little boy Adam's life. The vid showed that, you did not in fact, bend down to pick it up off the deck during the riot or murder anyone. And I also saw, but didn't appreciate," Furman planted an irritated gawp on Amanda, then rotated her displeased look back to Jennifer, "Amanda shape-shift, or whatever you call it, from the entry hatch, snagged my hand comp, then returned to the hatch before I could yell at her to stop!"

Judge Furman's miffed ogle intensified in Amanda's direction again.

"…Then you did it again just to prove what I saw, or rather didn't see, was real!" The Judge eyeballed Nace warily.

"I now fully understand why you got me out of my rack early to conduct this trial, *Captain* Notchins." Furman squinted at Nace's new captain stripes hastily pinned on her shoulders. "I still don't know how you magically got promoted since yesterday but *that* is for another time."

Furman pinned Jennifer with an indignant scowl.

"Bane, I'm certain you had a hand in all this but everything in *my* courtroom requires proof. Proof that you demonstrated using Amanda to snatch up my hand comp twice without me knowing it. Even though I told Amanda I didn't want her touching my stuff a second time BECAUSE I'M NOT STUPID AND WITNESSED HER WHOOSHIE-SPOOSHIE DASH THE FIRST TIME!"

The testy tension on Furman's face vanished as quick as it appeared.

"On a lighter note," an edgy, reluctant corner of Furman's mouth lifted, "I appreciate the diversion. You three have no idea what it's like sitting here day after day watching the endless parade of human debris drift past me. You don't have to decide whether to lock people up, or release them back on-station, so that they can commit some other hideous offense."

Before a matching grin could form on the three women standing in front of Furman, the judge cleared her throat not liking any of their presumptive crap.

"Case dismissed!"

References:

- Dimitri's marriage proposal inspired by the song Feel The Impact. Written, Produced and Performed by Gen. Third Stone from the Middle / WB Music Corp. (ASCAP)